TRANSIENT

The Tommy Bookmark Story

Milton J Southerland

The characters in this story are entirely fictional and do not represent any individual or collective person living or dead. Any such resemblance is purely coincidental and unintentional.

The town is imaginary although similar to my hometown of Chatsworth, Georgia. The old historical Wright Hotel made a strong impression on the author and attempting to imagine the goings on there in days gone by contributed to the plot.

Published in the United States of America. 2008

ISBN 978-0-578-02234-5

Introduction

The town had everything. A major highway passing in front of the courthouse. A railroad passed along the back of the town at the foot of a beautiful mountain. Farming provided plenty of revenue for the surrounding county. Business men had high hopes for their new city. A wide street ran by the courthouse to the railroad.

A doctor read about the new town from reading an out-of-town newspaper. He had saved his money from a successful practice. Now he longed for a fresh start. His idea was to build a hotel and practice medicine, as well as, reside in the same building. Income would be generated in several ways. He was a good doctor with a likeable bedside manner. So, he felt sure his medical practice would grow. The hotel would pay for itself and provide additional income. A fine kitchen would be included with a reasonable charge for meals.

The doctor acquired some land along the wide street running through town to the railroad. The real estate was prime property. The city government gave him a break on his taxes at his request. After all, the hotel would benefit the town as much as it would him.

So the beautiful structure became a reality. It had several stories and a wraparound porch for his guest to lounge on during their stay. They could see the train depot and the courthouse from the porch facing the wide street. He was sure that they would enjoy all the goings on.

There were a couple of problems: Europe was at war and the bole weevil was on its way

Chapter

1

The red brick structure stood majestically under the shade of old oak trees. A spacious yard surrounded the tall building which reached toward the sky for three stories. A giant of a building, challenged only by the courthouse.

The first stop for any visitor must be the fresh-water well sprouting up from the wraparound porch. The wooden bucket usually sat full of freshly drawn water with a dipper hanging from its side. It was customary to get a little water in the dipper and slosh it around to rinse the previous users saliva away. A green spot in the grass highlighted the obvious place to toss the rinse water. Then, the visitor would take a drink in his mouth and spit it into the yard thus rinsing the road dust or whatever from his mouth. The ladies could get a glass to use if they desired. The smart ones availed themselves of this benefit. Finally, the visitor was ready to fill the dipper and drink the refreshing well water. A drop of water hung from the bottom of the dipper, usually falling off as they drank, often taking an indirect route across the drinker's chin. The sweet taste of the water kept their attention as they drank, so the occasional drop falling to their shirt was ignored. Some nicely dressed patrons would lean over the edge of the porch to avoid the dripping of the water or hold one hand under the dipper.

There was a rectangular shaped table against the wall with a tin wash basin on it. A separate bucket of water was beside the basin for washing hands and faces. Sweet smelling soap laid in a dish on the table. The towel was an adventure in itself. It hung on the wall over the little table. The doctor believed in good hygiene and had the towel replaced often. Even so, it was never quit clean after the first use. Some visitors would take one look at the towel and reach in their pocket for a handkerchief to wipe away the excess water. Others choose to just sling their hands and to wipe their faces on their sleeves. Even with all the little hazards, the stop at the well was a pleasant one.

With some of the road dust removed and dry throats satisfied for the moment, the visitor walks into the reception area and is greeted by a clerk who has been anticipating their entry. Since the well was outside his window, he could size up his customers before they came inside. The nicely dressed clerk smiles and greets the visitor. Then he pushes a book across the counter for the visitor to sign. After the financial part of the visit is settled, the clerk flips up a section of his counter and picks up the visitor's bags. The bags could be in many forms but the clerk was beyond surprise. He handled all the bags with care. He knew that a paper sack might contain a jar of precious preserves. A box might hold an expensive clock. The list was endless, so he handled them all as if they were delicate eggs.

There is just enough time to look around the lobby area and spot the door to the dining room. The clerk heads up the stairs to the second floor. The wood on the steps and rails is polished to a high gloss. The steps creak giving the visitor the feeling of being on an old ship. The solid door swings open on quiet hinges. Following the clerk inside, the visitor finds a spacious room with a bed large enough to accommodate the largest of patrons. The dresser and mirror reveal the work of a master craftsman. A pitcher and basin with a small mirror are provided for bathing. A chiffonier served as the closet. It, too, had a small mirror in the door. Near the window, sat an overstuffed chair just waiting for the visitor to relax with a book or gaze out upon the town. A door led to the balcony porch which was shaded by several large old oak trees. The balcony porch was lined with wicker furniture for the patrons convenience.

A visitor might hear the dinner bell about this time. It was the signal that the meal would be served in about fifteen minutes. A slam of the outhouse door reminds the visitor that a trip out that way would be appropriate before sitting down for a meal. A discreet door in the back of the hotel, on the ground floor, allows for an easy exit to the little building. There are actually two of the conveniences, both at a respectful distance from the hotel and each other. The men's outhouse was brown with a black shingle roof. The ladies' powder room was white with blue trim. It also had a black shingle roof. Several bags of lime were stacked beside the buildings. Two patches of green healthy grass indicated that they had been moved in the not too distant past. Inside the men's building were the usual necessities, a stack of old catalogs. Whatever is in the ladies' building is their business. The men always let the door slam on their way out, apparently to make some sort of announcement to the community. Usually, the ladies would hold the door to let it shut gently, then walk with their eyes watching their feet until they were clear of the trail to the little white building. A trip to the wash basin followed this adventure and dinner was served.

The dining area was just a big room with a long table running down the center. Copies of famous paintings circled the room, so that wherever one sat, some refinement and appreciation of a higher culture could be enjoyed. Bread and the various plates of food were placed strategically on the table but it was still necessary to ask someone to pass this and that. "Would you pass the biscuits?" "Could I have a spoon of those taters?" Or someone would ask for potatoes. However they said it, there seemed to be no language barrier around the big table. Conversations would break out here and there around mouthfuls of food. The women would usually talk quietly to someone sitting beside them. While the men seemed to find the person furthest from them to be the most interesting to talk to. So a crisscross of conversation invariably broke out at the meals. The doctor usually sat quietly at the head of the table but occasionally offered some tidbit of information to clear up a point. He could be very stern if the discussions got out of hand. A man once hit his fist on the table which brought the good doctor to his feet. "I will thank you sir to not hit your fist on the table. We do not want food splashed on the ladies." His cautions elicited a mumbled apology. If not, and the patron continued to make his point using the law of physics, some one of the other men would reinforce the good doctor's kind instructions. Whether out of respect for the doctor, or fear of missing the rest of the meal, we will never know. Once the cook came out to have her say. "I got a cake arisin' in the oven. Quit all that bangin' or I will let the dogs have it." She said wiping her hands on her apron and daring the man to challenge her authority. He looked at her sheepishly and blushed all the way down his neck. "Can we have a piece of the cake?" He asked her. She became very motherly then and replied, "Sure you can have a piece of cake but you got to finish your dinner first." "Yes ma'am" was his reply.

Back in the kitchen she gently opened the stove door and stuck a fork into the cake. It was just about done. She started beating up some icing to go with the fresh strawberry topping. Mary enjoyed her cooking and her sampling of the dishes, as was evident from her rounded appearance. She had designed the kitchen, right down to the sink and pump and the black stove with white doors. She had agreements with local gardeners and farmers to supply her kitchen on a regular basis. She paid them well and received only the best. If she ran across a bad item, she would show it to the supplier who would cower with embarrassment. "You know better than that John." She might say. "I'm sorry Miss Mary, that one slipped by me." "That's alright, John. Come to supper some night." "I will Miss Mary, thank you." They were all good friends but Mary's kitchen came first in her life. She always said that if you wanted to have a good meal, you had to have good fixin's to start with. Mary had two girls who helped her at meal times. They would fill and refill the glasses and watch for empty bowls. The girls were shy but real good at their work. It would not have been wise for anyone to say something 'off-handed' to her girls.

While the dishes rattle in the kitchen, a visitor would be served coffee or tea and some cake on the wraparound porch. The men would gather around the corner to use their tobacco or continue conversations started around the table. The ladies sat with backs straight and sipped their tea or coffee while trying not to hear the occasional profane remark from around the corner.

Into this atmosphere, we step with our story of people in a small town with large ideas. It is a world of local people stopping for a good meal. Of those who work hard to make their visit special. Then there are those who are passing through town or just hanging around for reasons of their own. Individually, we know them as the transient.

Chapter

2

One of the farmers tied his work horse in the shade while he was letting his meal settle. The horse stood quietly with an occasional swish at a fly with his tail. His head hung low and lazy. The big eyes drooping, heavy with sleep.

A car came down the wide street after turning off of the Georgia Turnpike. The driver waited until he got where he was going to apply the brakes. The motor adjusted to the sudden stop with a loud backfire out the tailpipe. Those dozing on the wraparound porch jumped from the noise and spilled anything they were holding, onto themselves or the porch. Mary came to the window to see what the commotion was all about. The doctor stood in the doorway near the clerks counter holding his reading glasses between his fingers.

A stout looking man exited the car just as the farmer's horse gave the fender a mighty kick. The man ran around to that side of his car and tried to give the big horse a shove away from the car. The horse did not move a step. The man squeezed into the small space between the horse and car to inspect the damage. He bent over to take a better look. The horse, already upset, took the opportunity to take a bite at the target presented him. The man straightened and leaped onto his car, then to the other side. The horse dropped his head and went back to his daydreams about hay and things.

The farmer came down off the porch to try to apologize to the man but he would have none of it. The farmer's name was

Bill. Bill tried to explain that the horse was an ornery old cuss and that he was worth all the trouble he caused because of the work he could do. The man from the car did not appreciate the horse's abilities. He demanded satisfaction for the damages to his car. Bill was slow to anger, like the good book said to be, but his neck was getting red from trying to hold his temper.

"Mister, I do not have any cash money. I can pay you off in eggs and a sack of po'taters." Bill said.

The man from the car started to walk back and forth, rubbing his behind, right in front of the ladies, one of which was the farmer's wife.

"Mister, if you can help it, you need to stop rubbing your behind in front of my wife and the rest of the ladies. It's a might embarrassing." Bill said.

The man stopped rubbing but said. "It's a might painful, too." He rolled his lips back over his upper teeth to poke a little fun at the way Bill expressed himself. By now, Bill had moved to within snatching distance of the man from the car. The man was still pacing but when he turned around the last time he butted into Bill's chest. It seemed to make him even madder when he realized he was not the biggest man around. He tried to push off from Bill with his hands against Bill's chest. He went back a ways but Bill did not move.

"Now, I don't want any trouble. I am sorry my horse hurt your car. I will trade out the damages, if you want me to. Besides that, there just ain't nothing else I can do." Bill said.

"Well, there is something I can do." The man said as he took a swing at Bill's exposed chin. His fist hit the big jaw causing Bill's head to jerk slightly to one side. He drew back for another swing but before he could Bill grabbed him by his shoulders and set him on his own car hood. They heard the booming voice behind them at the same time and both men turned to see who was talking.

"My wife said there was something going on down here at the hotel. I guess she was right. What's the problem?" Sheriff

Harley Singletree asked as he belched on his own stomach full of dinner. Sheriff Harley, as they called him, was a pretty big fellow but his belly hung over his belt as he walked with a 'it don't matter to me' swagger. Many mistook him for a pushover. To their surprise, would-be-criminals found him to be very strong under his layer of flab.

The man from the car spoke first. "This fat hillbilly let his horse kick my car and I want satisfaction."

"Bill maybe could be called a hillbilly but that is not fat you are looking at, except maybe between his ears." The sheriff said.

"Now Harley, you got no call to talk about me like that." Bill said.

"Don't get all red-in-the-neck again Bill. I was just trying to calm you men down." Sheriff Singletree told him.

"Just what I needed. A hick town where everybody is just one big happy family." The man said.

"Listen young man. We ain't always happy and some of us ain't no kin, but if you are looking for trouble I can help you with that little problem. My jail just happens to be empty." The sheriff said.

"But what about my car?" The man asked.

"Anybody knows you don't park a car next to a spirited animal. If I had been standing there half asleep, I would have kicked your car too. Haven't you ever been around a horse?" Harley asked him.

"Yes, I have been around horses. All they do is eat and make a stink. I find them very disgusting." He said.

"My horse don't stink any more than other animals except for the necessities and he can't help that." Bill said.

"Bill, would you back up a few feet until your neck goes back to its normal color. I don't want you to forget yourself. Now, go on, back up." The sheriff said stepping between the two men. Bill backed up into the shade in front of his horse.

"His car is dented, Bill, can you make that good?" Harley asked.

"I offered him some eggs and a sack of po'taters. He thought it was funny." Bill said.

"Sounds fair to me." The sheriff said.

"Not to me. I need cash to get my car fixed." The man insisted.

"Cash is scarce around these parts." The sheriff said while he scratched his head. Just when he was ready to give up on a solution, the doctor came to his rescue.

"How much to get your car fixed?" The doctor asked.

"At least twenty dollars, if I shop around." The man told him.

"Well, you shop around. Here is your twenty. Give the sheriff a receipt as payment in full for all damages." He turned to Bill. "I will take those eggs and potatoes off your hands."

"Thanks Doc. I will throw in some extra to make it up to twenty dollars. Mister I'm sorry about your car." Bill turned to walk back to his perch on the porch. The doctor was dwarfed, by the big farmer, as he also walked back to the hotel.

"Well, young man, I expect you will be moving on now." The sheriff said.

"No sir. I have business in town." He said.

"Okay, your business is your business, but if you are staying around town long, you best mind your manners." He advised.

The young man carried his bag to the clerks desk to check in. The clerk was his usual friendly self. He had seen the disagreement outside but still kept his professional demeanor. He escorted the young man upstairs to his room. He wanted a room on the front so he could watch his car.

A door was open and the young man saw the doctor bent over a woman lying in bed. She glowed with radiance.

"Is that the doctor's wife?" The young man inquired.

"His patient." The clerk replied.

"They seem happy to see each other." The young man said

rather facetiously.

"You best keep those thoughts to yourself. She is an invalid. The doctor takes care of her." The clerk said.

"Why should I be afraid of a doctor?" The young man asked.

"He owns the building." The clerk replied with satisfaction.

The clerk went over the many amenities of the hotel and left the guest to look around. He lost his smile as soon as his back was turned to the difficult man. He passed by the room where the doctor and the lady were talking. The door was still open so he lifted a hand in greeting. The lady smiled and lifted a feeble hand. She breathed in deeply and called out to him in a hushed voice.

"Hello Robert. You're a good boy. I've been praying for you." She said looking past the doctor who had turned his head toward Robert.

"Thank you Miss Alice." He said and went back to his perch behind the front desk.

"He is such a fine boy." Miss Alice told the doctor.

"Yes he is, but he is twenty-five years old. They like to be called men at that age." The doctor corrected.

"Well, he is a boy to me. I am old enough to be his mother. I didn't mean any offense." She said.

"And he took no offense. He loves you as much as I do." The doctor said.

"Your wife will get you for that kind of talk." She warned.

"She is not the jealous type. Besides, most of her male patients fall in love with her. It is a normal thing between patient and nurse." He explained.

"Oh, I know all that Will. You talk to me like I was a school girl. It is not my mind that is sick. It's my body." She

said.

Doctor Will T. Hill had found Miss Alice alone in her home except for the body of her dead husband. He had died instantly of a heart attack. He had worked his farm during the day and cared for Miss Alice day and night. He was a strong man but the years without sufficient sleep and worry over his beloved took a tremendous toll on his heart. He found Miss Alice praying that someone would happen by so her husband could be properly taken care of. She could see him in the kitchen but could not move to help him. It was a hard time for her. Doctor Hill took her in his arms and brought her, immediately, to the hotel where his wife Bertha took charge.

"I will take care of this poor thing. You go on out and make the arrangements for her husband." Bertha told him.

"I am not a poor thing." Miss Alice said. "My husband just went to heaven ahead of me. I will catch up to him."

"Yes, Miss Alice. I just wanted to reassure my husband. He worries about everything." Bertha told her.

"I know my dear. You both are so kind. I will of course sell the farm to pay my way here at the hotel." Miss Alice said.

"We can take care of that later. Let's just get you cleaned up for now." Bertha said taking charge.

Miss Alice had been a model patient. She read her Bible and prayed most of the time. She could often be heard singing hymns from the song book she kept on the table beside her Bible. She did not like to be patronized, so they all talked to her openly and honestly. She did the same.

"What happened outside?" She asked the doctor coming back to the present.

"Some young fellow parked too close to Bill's horse. His car got kicked." Doctor Hill said.

"I guess the horse had a right to defend himself." Miss Alice said.

"I guess he did." The doctor said laughing. He got up to take care of other business.

The doctor left Miss Alice to her prayers and went to the register downstairs.

"Who is that young man you just took upstairs?" He asked.

Robert looked at the register. "He signed in as Lawrence Aulding from Atlanta."

"We will just have to keep an eye on Mister Aulding." Doctor Hill said.

"Yes sir." Robert said to the doctor's back. He had already headed upstairs to his third floor office. The office was small but had an adjoining examination room. As the doctor sat behind his desk he was facing the wall of the examination room. Turning to his left he could see the railroad depot. To his right was the hallway with his living quarters on the other side. Behind him were his medical books. He studied from medical journals, as well as, the herbal remedies which he used when modern medicine failed. In his spare time, he always searched for something to help Miss Alice. He longed to see her on her feet again. He had used soaking baths in herbs of various combinations. She had found some relief from pain but still gained no strength in her body. He suspected that her heart was just too weak to support her system. He fell asleep with his wire-rimmed glasses still perched on his nose.

"Doctor Hill. It is time for supper." Bertha said while gently patting his shoulder. She reached for his glasses and laid them atop the open book he had been studying.

They gathered around the table for the evening meal. Usually, only the hotel guest showed up for the supper. The people from out in the county were already home for the day. They would be doing the evening chores of slopping the hogs and milking the cows. Maybe they would work in their gardens in the cool of the evening.

Doctor Hill looked around the table. The young Mister Aulding sat down the table, on his right. Miss Alice had been brought down to sit on his left. Bertha sat to his right. Sheriff

Singletree and his wife joined them. Two other guest had
checked in while he was upstairs. One was a Baptist preacher
in town to check on the possibilities of establishing another
church. The other was a strong looking fellow in a store
bought suit. He was not real talkative about what he did but
he was a friendly sort. Mary did her usual fine job, serving
them as if they were royalty. The two girls going discreetly
around the table to refill glasses and replace empty bowls.

One of the girls was named Marsha. She happened to be
the most mature of the two. She spotted an empty bowl in
front of Mister Aulding, reached to get it and hurried off to
the kitchen for more potatoes. She came back, momentarily,
and reached between Mister Aulding and the young man in
the store bought suit to put the bowl on the table. Mister
Aulding turned slightly to allow her more room. As she
stretched between them, he let his hand fall to her waist,
suspiciously close to her hips. She jerked back leaving the
bowl spinning on the table. Her face turned scarlet as she
stood backed up against the wall. The young man in the suit
was quick to react. He brought his left hand up and caught
the wrist of Mister Aulding. Using his body strength, he
turned in his chair, sending Mister Aulding over on his back,
still in his chair.

"We do not take liberties with ladies, Mister Aulding." He
said, now standing over him.

Doctor Hill was standing on Mister Aulding's other side.
Mister Aulding looked up to see two very angry men.

"That is two mistakes, Mister Aulding, one more and you
are out of this hotel." The doctor said.

Sheriff Singletree was chewing on an ear of corn. He
stopped for a moment when he saw what Aulding did but the
young man in the suit handled things to fast for him to get up.
Mister Aulding got up and resumed his place at the table. He
looked at the sheriff for some possible intervention but he just
smiled around his cob of corn.

"Aren't you going to do anything?" Mister Aulding asked.

"People have been shot for what you did. You came out pretty good." Sheriff Singletree said. A few grains of corn slipped from his mouth and fell to his plate. A lady beside him looked his way.

"Sorry ma'am. I never could sheriff and eat at the same time." He said.

Brother Paul Newton sat in silence observing the play as it unfolded before him. People were a joy to watch. If he had been in the young man's place, with the suit, he would have done the same thing. You just did not go around touching decent young ladies on their behind. Mister Aulding would have to be a model citizen the rest of his stay or he might find himself tied to a tree out in the country.

Mister Aulding looked around the table. He saw no friends. Mary, the cook, stood sideways in the kitchen doorway until she caught his eye. She was holding a rolling pin. Mary did not look at all happy. Marsha continued to serve throughout the meal but she was nervous and flushed. She jumped when anyone moved their hand if she was anywhere close by.

Chapter

3

Hatsworth City was set for prosperity, the railroad being built through in 1905. The little spat with Spain established the muscle of the United States on an international level, if all the other bloodletting had not already accomplished that feat. Cotton was grown in every strip of land where a rock could be moved to make room for the seeds. The local red dirt made good bricks but who would have believed cotton would love it too. The clay turned to dust if the weather was dry and to glue if it rained but somehow the cotton stalk drew the right ingredients from the soil to make white boles of a precious commodity. The bole weevil would come later like an Egyptian plague.

The young man who corrected Mister Aulding at the supper table, sat on the porch drinking coffee long after sundown. He thought the doctor might come down for some fresh air before going to bed. He was right. He waited for the doctor to notice him then went over for a chat.

"Doctor. My name is Tommy Bookmark. I have just finished college up north. I wanted to get to know the culture of the south so I can better understand the causes of the Civil War. It is for a historical novel I plan to write someday. Do you know where I could get some actual work on a farm?"

"Nice to meet you Mister Bookmark. With a name like that, you should write a novel. About the work, Bill McNeill raises cotton and corn in the upper part of the county. He mentioned that he could use some help. He just has the one daughter. She is a hard worker but she can only do so much. You met her today, in a way, she was the waitress you rescued." Doctor Hill said.

"Why does she work here, if there is so much to do on the farm?" Bookmark asked.

"One word. Cash. She gets paid cash for her work here which helps the family buy things they can't grow on the farm." The doctor told him.

"I see. Can you draw me a map to his place?" He asked.

"Sure. I will have it for you at breakfast." Doctor Hill said.

"What do you think about the war in Europe? Will we get involved?" Bookmark asked.

"We will be in it very soon. We will probably have to go over and tilt the scales." The doctor said simply.

"War sure is a waste of humanity." Bookmark said, a tinge of anger in his voice.

"The people who start them sit back in their castles and send the young to defend their honor. In the old days, the leader of the war was out front with the troops." Doctor Hill commented.

"Well, I will go off to bed before I get too mad to sleep. Goodnight Doctor. Thank you for the conversation." Mister Bookmark said.

"Goodnight young man."

True to his word, the doctor handed Mister Bookmark a detailed map showing how to get to Bill McNeil's farm. He also included some of the surrounding county. Mary heard he might not be back for dinner so she packed him a lunch. Bookmark had decided to keep his room so he could have it for the weekends when he was not working.

Mister Bookmark packed some work clothes and went out to crank his 1914 Model T Ford Runabout. The one he had was equipped with electric lights instead of the gas lamps. He liked the car. He could fold the windshield in if he needed a breeze. Once he drove one with a foldout windshield and almost wrecked trying to work it while driving. The windshield on his car was no problem to let down while driving.

He drove up the federal road following his map to the turnoff. He was glad to get the tip on the job but rather happy that Marsha would be there too. Real happy as a matter-of-fact.

Tommy found his way to the farm without any trouble. He drove between rows of white fields of cotton. The road was dusty and sent up a cloud as he drove to the farmhouse. There was a wooden bridge near the house which crossed a small creek. The stream gurgled over rocks which shined like gems in the crystal clear water. The farmhouse was white with a dusting from the fields. The soil was not so red here in the upper part of the county. There was a barn connected to the pasture which bordered the sprawling fields of cotton and corn. Other outbuildings completed the picture.

The hour was late for a farmer. Bill and Marsha were already out in the fields someplace. Mrs. McNeil was at the clothesline hanging out her laundry. She saw him coming and hoped he slowed down so her clothes would not get dusty. He did slow down and made a friend in Mrs. McNeil before he even arrived at the house. She greeted him with a clothespin in her mouth. He smiled his best smile then told her his business. She directed him down a road beside the pasture fence to where her husband and daughter were working.

He found the place easy enough. There was a tractor with a large trailer attached. The sides of the trailer were grated metal so he could see that cotton was already piling up inside. In the midst of the never ending rows of white was a section of brown where the cotton had been picked. Stretched out in a zigzag row were the cotton pickers. Each grabbing at the stalks of cotton with practiced fingers. Tommy walked down the rows of empty stalks. He learned quickly to raise his hands above the stalks. If he held them by his side, the empty cotton boles scratched the backs of his hands. There were spurs where the boles had opened and dried.

Tommy found Bill lagging behind the other more youthful pickers. He soon discovered why. Bill was picking three rows while they picked one. Bill was a big man. So instead of bending over the rows, he straddled one on his knees and picked one on either side. He would pick until he had a large handful of cotton then roll it back into his picksack. Tommy stopped before he got to the group. He was amazed at their precision with the task. The hands darted from bole to bole with the skill of a speed typist. He also saw Marsha, intent on her work. A wisp of hair fell from her hat and dangled in front of her face.

Tommy walked to a position on the outside row of cotton Bill was working on. Bill hesitated for just a moment when Tommy spoke, then continued his picking. Tommy explained his situation and his desires. He was honest about his inexperience.

"Marsha takes care of teaching the new workers." He said.

He called Marsha over to where he still reached for the white fluffs of cotton in rapid motions. She removed her picksack from around her shoulders and maneuvered between the rows of cotton. She held one hand at the small of her back as she slowly straightened to her full height. She wiped perspiration back with the single strand of hair using the back of her long sleeve.

"Mister Bookmark has never picked cotton. He will be staying with us until the harvest is finished. Please teach him how to pick cotton the right way." Bill said.

"Come with me, please." Marsha told Tommy.

They walked to the big trailer where she picked out a picksack that had no holes. She showed him the twist of wire at the corner which was used for weighing.

"You get three cents a pound. If there are any stalks or boles in the cotton, we may dock you a few pounds. We have had people put rocks in to get more weight. Those people are sent home. The rocks could cause a fire at the gin. Other than that, the main rule is 'do not gooselock'." She said as she walked to a stalk that still had cotton on it. She reached for the boles of cotton with delicate fingers. The cotton disappeared from the stalk into her hands and was shuffled into the cradle of her wrist as she picked. When she was finished, she pointed at the stalk she had just picked, then at one across the way that had also been picked clean.

"Do you see the difference?" She asked.

"Yes. The one you just did has little bits of cotton in some of the boles." Tommy said.

"Those are gooselocks." She said. "If you do a whole row

like that, it will stand out a mile away. At first, you will have to reach back in and pull the bits you leave behind. After a while, you will learn how to pick without leaving them."

"I understand." Tommy said.

"We will start two new rows. I will help you if you get behind." Marsha said as she picked out an empty sack.

Side-by-side they worked. He was finishing up his first stalk of cotton and looked over to see if Marsha had any comments. She was not there. Marsha had picked her row well ahead of him. Now she had crossed over her row of cotton and was picking both his and hers. He worked hard to pick the row up to where she had started picking both rows. Then he dragged his small load of cotton up to where she was working.

"I am not doing very well. Am I?" he asked.

"You are doing fine. Let me see your fingers." She said.

He held out his hands obediently. Blood formed around the back of his fingernails where the spurs on the cotton boles had stuck them.

"Do it like this." She demonstrated letting her fingers close over the white cotton. He had been jamming his fingers into the bole thus pricking his fingers. She closed her fingers over the cotton letting her fingers trail between the spurs.

"I think I got it." He said and tried the technique.

"You are doing just fine Mister Bookmark." She stopped picking for just the slightest moment. "Thank you for helping me at the hotel."

"You are welcome. I did not think you remembered me." He replied.

"I remember." She said and bent over the row of cotton seeming to make it magically disappear from the stalks.

Tommy bent to the task. He lost himself in the world of white. Finally he noticed that his picksack was starting to cut into his shoulder. He was making progress at last. He glanced down the row to where Marsha was packing in a last handful of cotton into her sack. She stood it on end and let the flap fall over the top. Then, as if it was no trouble at all, she gave the sack of cotton a flip with her knee bringing it to rest on her shoulder. She walked past him with it balanced on her shoulder.

"I could have gotten that for you." He said as she went by.

"We mostly carry our own cotton. It is only a hundred pounds. I do not lift much more than that. Come on. We need to weigh-up, it is dinner time. We will eat at the house." She said smiling.

Tommy shook his cotton down and stood the sack on its end like he had seen Marsha do. He gave it a flip to get it onto his shoulder. It did not work quiet so well for him. He got too much weight behind him and the sack of cotton pulled him across two rows of cotton before he fell down. He sheepishly climbed to his feet and picked up his cotton in a less dramatic manner. Marsha saw him fall and hid her smile underneath her wide brimmed hat. She had seen that happen a thousand times.

"Keep your cotton packed tight." She told him with a straight face when he got to the scales. "It rides better on your shoulder."

A table was spread under the shade of great old trees in the yard behind the kitchen. They gathered around the table with Mister McNeil at the head. His wife sat by his right side. Tommy reached for something close to his plate but Marsha pulled his hand down by his sleeve. Mister McNeil looked up from his bowed head to see if he had everyone's attention. Then, in a humble and straightforward manner, he thanked the Lord for all the food, the good weather and the help he had provided to gather in his crops. His Amen was a 'go' signal for the workers. They began filling their plates and passing the bowls around the table. The meal was as good as Tommy had eaten anywhere. He ate so much that all he could think about was taking a nap. Marsha ate quietly at his side. She was apparently to be his mentor in the ways of the farm. On his first mornings work, he had picked fifty pounds of cotton and made a buck-fifty. The meal was worth much more than his wages.

Not knowing what else to do, he sat under the shade and let his eyelids get heavy. He did not sleep but he just as well have, for he drifted in a land between sleep and consciousness. He saw Marsha help with clearing the table. Then, she was at the well drawing water into several large tubs. The other pickers were stirring, so he got to his feet and waited. One hour to the second they loaded up for the ride back to the field. Marsha cheerfully jumped into her place.

"Don't you ever rest?" He asked.

"Sure. Mama does not have any help at the house though, so I help her all I can." Marsha said.

"You are amazing." Tommy said.

"No. Mister Bookmark. I am just a farm girl." She said.

He determined to not let her down. He got off the trailer and attacked his row of cotton. His back hurt but he did not straighten to stretch. His fingers bleed but he wiped them on his pants and kept picking. He was rewarded with the strap of his picksack digging into his shoulders. It was quitting time and he could not pack another handful into the sack. Marsha had walked past him several times with her sack packed full but he kept working. Now, he shouldered his load of cotton and only stumbled across one row of cotton before he got it balanced. He was getting better. He weighed up at a hundred and ten pounds.

"You did good Mister Bookmark." Bill said. That was all he had said all afternoon.

Marsha had walked from the field an hour earlier. Later, Tommy heard the farm truck leave the house and saw dust on the long driveway. She had left to work at the hotel during the evening meal. The other pickers were from neighboring houses so they walked off in various directions for their short walks home. Each of them had their own special shortcuts through the fields or down the drive.

Bill showed Tommy where he would sleep. It was a closed

in room on the back porch.

"I have some chores to do before supper." Bill said. "We eat supper when Marsha gets home. You can wash up down at the creek."

"I would like to help with the chores, if I could. I don't expect any pay for that. The room and board is enough." Tommy offered.

Tommy wrestled with bales of hay and bags of mix for the hogs. He worked twice as hard as was necessary to do the job but he was learning. Mister McNeil appreciated his enthusiasm and showed him little tips here and there. Finally, he got a change of clothes and walked down to the creek. He found where the water had been dammed up to make it waist deep on him. He plunged in and soothed his aching muscles. Bill had given him a bar of homemade soap to use as long as it lasted. He scrubbed off the dirt of a hard days work. Soon, he heard the old farm truck coming down the driveway. He was hidden from sight but still hurried to dress. He did not have a towel so his clothes soaked up the water that remained on him. He was soon warm again in the warm humid air.

Tommy made his way back to the house. Marsha met him at the door and invited him to the kitchen for supper.

"We eat inside when its just us." Marsha said.

"I am intruding." Tommy said, not feeling bold enough to be considered part of 'us'.

"Nonsense." She said leading the way through the house to the kitchen. It was a large room used for cooking and eating. Tommy waited for Bill to give thanks before he did any reaching. When the prayer was finished, Marsha held a bowl for him. He scooped out a good portion and she passed it up the table. There was just the four of them making Tommy feel a little awkward. He soon relaxed, though, as the family discussed their daily activities. Mrs. McNeil was interested in all the 'goings on' around the farm. She spent her day working at the house and enjoyed the little while she could spend with her family. Tommy soon joined in with his exploits in the cotton field. They all had a good laugh. It was where they had all started on their first day in the field. Marsha finished up hurriedly. She excused herself and went to her room to grab a change of clothes. As she came back by the kitchen door she spoke to her Mama.

"I will help with dishes as soon as I get back from the creek." She said and she was out the door running. She had to get her bath before dark. The sun was already disappearing. Bill got up.

"I got milking to do, if you want to come along." He said. Tommy followed him. He wondered if these people ever stopped working.

"Do you always work like this?" Tommy asked.

"Mostly." Bill replied. "We slow down some when it rains. I hope we are dry for a spell yet. A hard rain would beat the cotton right out on the ground."

Tommy realized that they were racing against an uncertain clock. Whether or not they did good on their crops depending on getting it harvested before the weather changed. He decided he would take two rows at a time in the morning. As the milk bucket filled under Bill's practiced milking, Tommy heard Marsha giggle past the barn toward the house. The water must have been really chilly. By the time the milking was finished, they had two cows for milking, Marsha had her hair rolled and was helping with the dishes.

"I will say goodnight." Tommy told them.

"Don't forget to blow out the kerosene lamp. You probably noticed the power lines don't come out this far yet." Marsha said.

"Okay. Thanks." He said.

A chorus of goodnights followed him out the door. He was a little embarrassed to be made part of the family so quickly. He would look back later to realize that was their way around here. He would be trusted as long as he gave no reason to be treated otherwise. He wrote in his journal for a few minutes and laid back on his pillow. He awoke with a start and blew out the lamp. He had almost forgotten.

He went to sleep to the sound of Marsha and her Mama singing in the kitchen as they washed the last of the dishes. The little he heard before falling asleep sounded like *Blessed Assurance by Fanny Crosby (1873)*. Now what was that story he heard about soldiers using page numbers of hymnals as greetings?

A Mister Sanky had published a song book. The soldiers, in an earlier conflict, remembered the songs by page number. They had, in-fact, learned the songs so well that they could call out a page number and their fellow soldier would immediately recall the entire hymn. In one of the wars, men were passing each other in formation. One man called out a greeting to those passing the other way by using a page from the hymn book. It was Sanky's hymn page 494 which was *God will Take Care of You.* The man replied by saying 'six further on' meaning page 500 which was Crosby's *Blessed Assurance.*

Bill poured water into the wash pan on the back porch. He washed his face and hands and flipped the dirty water into the back yard. He banged the pan on the narrow table where it sat.

"I am going to do the milking. Breakfast is in twenty minutes. The sun will be up in thirty and should have the cotton dry an hour from now. See you at breakfast." Bill said laughing to himself on his way to the barn.

Tommy jumped up in bed and wondered where he was. He remembered a loud noise and a speech about when the sun came up. He looked out the small window and remembered he was on a farm. He threw on his clothes and stumbled to the outhouse, then to the barn. He leaned on the door frame of the stable where Bill was filling a bucket with milk.

"Over there is a bucket with some warm water in it. Wash her good and try your hand at milking." Bill said.

Tommy looked at Bill. He was sitting on a three-legged stool and going at it with both hands. Tommy looked around and found another stool. He cautiously went into the stable. The cow did not move but turned her head to see who was invading her stable. Tommy sat down ready to milk.

"Her leg is in the way." He yelled.

"Just give it a little nudge. She will move it." Bill answered.

Tommy did and she did. He started milking but was having little success. He turned to tell Bill but caught the cows tail in his face before he could speak. The tail was gone just as quick.

"She hit me." Tommy said.

"Just letting you know she is boss." Bill was finished and set his bucket out of harms way. "Here let me show you."

Bill gave Tommy a closeup demonstration of the technique. Tommy tried again and was more successful. Bill let him work at it until he got a few swats with the cow's tail.

"Let me finish for you. We got to get up to the house before breakfast gets cold." Bill said.

They carried the two buckets of milk to the house.

"Better leave your shoes on the porch. You will understand when it gets light out." Bill told him. "Wash your hands after you take them off. You will understand that 'why' later, also."

Breakfast was a delight like all the meals at the McNeil house. They had lost time with the cows so there was little talk. Everyone was taking their time eating but wasting none talking. Tommy did the same.

Marsha slipped out to the outhouse and was washing her hands when Tommy came out to put his shoes on. He barely had them tied when Marsha yelled at him.

"Race ya to the wagon!" She said.

He took off after her and immediately slipped in the slick grass where they had been throwing the excess wash water. He got up and followed her to the wagon. She was sitting there eating an apple, watching him wipe the mud from his hands.

"You better keep an eye on those two. They seem to be

hitting it off pretty well." Mrs. McNeil told her husband.

"I am watching them." He said gruffly.

"Tommy is a fine boy." She said.

"He is a grown man and don't know the first thing about farming. But he is the most determined young man I have ever seen." Bill said more gently.

"Marsha likes him." She said.

"She does? How can you tell?" Bill asked.

"I can tell." Mrs. McNeil said knowingly.

They had their morning kiss and Mrs. McNeil got a morning pinch. Bill ran ahead of the dish towel but managed a serious expression by the time he got to the wagon. "Let's go to work."

Chapter

4

Lawrence Aulding was not particularly happy being in this small town. The hotel was nice enough and the meals were some of the best he had ever eaten. He basically did not have a choice about being here. His boss had sent him up to organize the moonshine trade. He had a simple job, locate the moonshiner and offer him a deal he could not refuse. He would provide transportation and the purchase of a certain amount in exchange for exclusive rights to the product. A ten percent allowance would be made for local sales. So, how did he find the elusive illegal whiskey makers. He wondered.

For several days, Aulding hung out at the local grocery stores. He noted in a little book the purchases of the customers. The ingredients for the brew were: corn meal, sugar, water, yeast and malt (barley steeped in water until it sprouted). He supposed they could raise some of the ingredients but sugar was not a local crop. He figured it would be purchased at the most convenient place, the local grocery store. Sure, people used it for canning but not in the quantities he was watching out for. After he spent a few days in one store, he moved on to another. He cataloged the vehicles and tag numbers. It was a small thing for him to find out who owned them from his friends in the city. Soon, he had it narrowed down to a few possibilities.

Next, Aulding asked where the local grist mills were

located and staked them out. It was not easy to hide at the mills, so he hung around asking questions about how they did things until they got used to him being there. He told them he was from the city and did not know anything about such things. The operators were happy to show the city kid their expertise.

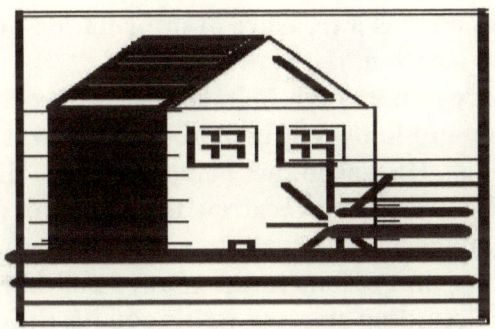

His expectation was correct. The same cars showed up at the mills to pickup meal or have corn ground while they waited. Patiently he plotted the activities and found that it was a regular routine. The men would make their rounds every week spreading the purchases around among the businesses in the county. It did not fool the millers for a minute but it did give them an excuse to not show suspicion. He accepted the various reasons for the large purchases as they were given. If no reason was offered, he knew not to ask for any. Occasionally, Aulding saw a brown paper sack being handed to the millers with a broad smile. Once a miller explained to Aulding that he did not drink but his wife used it for medicinal purposes in the winter. "It is good for coughs." He said.

Aulding talked to some of the pickup men on a casual basis. He asked no particular questions. He just wanted them to remember him as a city man. He also did not want them to mistake him for a revenue agent. He even took a drink or two of the whisky to incriminate himself against such an assumption. By partaking of the illegal mixture, he was making himself a party to the crime. And so, he worked his magic. His little book was a treasure of information on the local moonshine operation.

Aulding was arrogant enough to believe that his actions were totally secret and known only to himself. He was busy being inconspicuous. He was in fact being watched. His lack of purchases at the grocery stores drew the attention of the clerks and the managers. They were nervous about the sugar purchases, knowing that no one in the county did that much canning. So, when Aulding starting writing in his little book, the people at the stores suspected him of being a revenue agent. Although there were many religious people in the county who disapproved of the moonshine business and the preachers preached against the elixir, it was part of the local economy and outsiders were not welcome.   Sheriff Singletree would lock up an occasional moonshiner to let them know he was watching them. He kept them for a couple of days and let them go back to the mountains. Usually, one of their boys would make the rounds while the man was in jail. They even stopped by to bring the man some home cooking sent by his wife. She might write a note about the baby being a little sick or the cow getting out. They all knew the sheriff read the notes and so it was as much a note to him as to her husband. The sheriff being a soft-touch would invariably let them out early. The sheriff's wife had no comment about his soft-touch but the sheriff explained anyway.

"Well, his family needs him. He ain't got no education. I don't know what else he could do to support them. That land up there barely makes a garden, so he can't farm for a living.

Don't look at me that way. Just tell the boy to wait for his Pa. He can ride back with him." The sheriff told his wife.

She went to the kitchen to tell the boy to wait. He was busy eating as much of an apple pie as he could and did not appear to be leaving anytime soon. Truth was, his Mama had told him to wait around in case the sheriff was in a charitable mood. The boy was accustomed to the routine and so just nodded when the sheriff's wife told him to wait. His truck was parked in the jail parking lot loaded down with all the supplies they would need for the next batch of moonshine. The weather was good, so he had not bothered to cover the supplies with the old canvas they kept in the truck for that purpose. If the sheriff had looked out his window, he could have found cause to lock up the two of them. He did not look and knew better. He had no intention of finding a legal reason to keep the only two adults in the family in his jail while the cow ran loose and the baby cried. He knew he would not have been able to sleep with the boy and his daddy both upstairs behind bars. So, he did not look out his window for fear of what his practiced eyes would see.

"You boys better change your route. I could set a clock by you if I was a mind to." The sheriff told them.

"We will, Sheriff. Thanks for the good eatin' Mrs. Singletree." He told the sheriff's wife. She smiled and left her husband alone with the two men.

"There is a city man around town. He has been counting something down at the grocery stores. Just so you know. I do not want the federal boys swarming around my county. So, do not give them any reason. You make any bad whiskey and I will lock you both up and throw away the key." He said sternly.

"Okay Harley. We get the message. Thanks again for the good eatins'." The man said as he went to his truck.

"And use that canvas. What are you doing advertising?" The sheriff hollered out the door at them.

The man and his son pulled the canvas over their supplies

and drove off toward the hills.

"She sure can cook." The boy said.

"Yes, Son. She sure can." His daddy said. "But not as good as your Maw. You be sure and tell her that while your bragging on Mrs. Singletree's fixins'."

Aulding followed the truck as it left the jail. He was ready to make his first offer. Now might be a good time, since the sheriff had maybe shaken them up a little. Aulding did not know that spending time at the jail was as much a part of their routine as picking up the meal from the mill.

"There is someone following us." The boy said.

"I know. He will probably drown out at the next creek. We will back up and pull him out if he answers our questions right." Pa said. He hit the creek with the big truck wheels and parted the waters for their crossing. Aulding drove in easy-like and did fine until his tailpipe submerged. The car stalled in the middle of the creek.

The man backed his truck up to the creek and got out. He walked back to the edge of the water and looked at Aulding sitting in his car with water running out of the door and over his running boards.

"Looks like you are in a fix." The man said.

"Can you help me?" Aulding asked.

"Yes." The man said.

"Well." Aulding snapped.

"Don't snap at me young man. I've whipped my boy for that tone of voice. You asked me if I could help and I said yes. I did not say I would help." The man said.

"Will you help?" Aulding asked. "Please." He added after a pause.

"I reckon." The man said.

The boy got a rope and wadded out to the front bumper of the car. He looped the other end over the frame of the truck.

"Pull him out easy boy." The man told his son.

When the car was on dry land again, Aulding reached for the starter.

"Better let the water run out of that tailpipe. Meanwhile, we can have us a little talk." The man said.

"My name is Aulding. Lawrence Aulding. I have come to offer you a business proposition." Aulding said.

"I don't need none of that. You can turn around just up ahead. Hit the creek hard so you sort of float across. We will make sure you get across okay." The man said.

"May I ask your name?" Aulding asked.

"Sure." The man said.

"What is your name?" He asked exasperated. Most people would have just told him their name after the first question.

"My name is James Inkle. My boy's name is James too."

"Doesn't that get confusing?" Aulding asked.

"Not at home, just in town sometimes. They call me Pa at home." Mister Inkle informed him. "Now that turnaround is just up the road. I will get the boy to move the truck."

"Can we talk just a minute?" Aulding asked.

"You can talk. I'm finished." Inkle told him.

Aulding laid out his deal. He said he was prepared to pay a cash advance right on the spot. All Mister Inkle had to do was have the agreed on amount of brew placed on the other side of the creek for pickup at a certain time on a certain day.

"You can't rush the making of good whiskey." Inkle said.

"I know. We do not want you to rush. You tell me when to pickup the first load." Aulding said.

Mister Inkle did some calculating and set a date for the first pickup. Aulding handed over the cash money. Little James' eyes popped out when he saw the greenbacks. He had never touched one of his own, although he had taken some to the stores to pay for the makings. They moved the truck up the hill so Aulding could get turned around. He hit the creek like they told him and made it across. Big James handed Little James one of the green backs.

"Get yourself a new pair of shoes." He told him.

Little James was happy nearly to tears. He looked down at his bare feet. He had knots on his toes where he had banged them on everything from the chairs in the kitchen to the slop bucket. He smiled up at his dad.

"You can drive Son." Big James told him to drive more to keep him busy, so he wouldn't embarrass himself by crying, than anything else. He was a big tough lanky boy but he had a heart of mush. They drove up to the house. The baby was playing in the floor at Maw's feet. She seemed to be feeling better already.

Aulding went back to his hotel room for the evening. His plan was coming together nicely. He arrived just in time for supper. The usual crowd was there. The preacher looked his way and Aulding tried to stare him down but to no success. A new fellow was in the hotel. He looked like a salesman. He wore a nice suit and carried a hat in his hand. He was slim, tall and seemed to stoop to avoid the overhead. He was a quiet fellow with curly brown hair, blue eyes and a quick smile. His name was Ben Smith. Ben said he was on vacation and just wanted to enjoy the mountains for a while. That remark made such good sense that it stopped all wonder over what he was doing here.

Marsha and her friend served the meal almost invisibly, while the guest talked among themselves. The preacher was extra nice to Marsha's friend when he got the chance. She was as shy as Marsha. She wore her hair long but tied back during the meals. It was black. Her eyes were brown. She was shorter than Marsha and very petite. Her name was Mary.

Chapter

5

Paul Newton had quietly made his rounds in the
community. He visited the business owners in town, even the
sheriff. Then he made his way out to the surrounding farms.
The people were very receptive to his idea of starting a new
church. He found an old building and rented it for a modest
amount. He worked long hours to get it ready for his first
meeting. He set up what ever he could find for seats but
bought enough wood to make a pulpit. It was as ready as he
could get it for now.

Mary Wilmington and her family had promised to attend.
He wondered, seriously, if she would like his preaching. He
hoped so, for he had no intention of changing, even for her
approval.

Sunday morning came and the preacher stood at the door
to greet those who came. The turnout was good. Better than
he expected. Some of the farmers came to town and brought
their lunches. They would eat after church then return to
their homes. He had brought along a small hymn book for his
congregation to use. Getting up, he thanked them all again
for coming.

"Please turn to hymn number one." He said.

The congregation stood and turned to the first hymn in the
book. Most of them seemed to know the song and sang it out,

loud and clear. He led a few more then invited them to be seated. It was time to preach. He had no idea what they were expecting. Some would call him a country preacher. Others would call him loud. He did not try to put on a show or please anyone. He just preached like he had always preached. His voice carried well as he held his Bible aloft and quoted more than he read. The sermon was one of warning and love.

He started with Adam's sin and walked through the vile streets of Sodom. He told of David's anointing and his utter fall into disgrace. Then he softly stepped into Bethlehem and found a manger with a new born baby inside. He cried out the announcement by the angels to the shepherds watching their flock. He told about Jesus' perfect life and his terrible death for sinners. Then he told how Mary went to the tomb and found it empty. And very softly he said, "He did it all for you."

A long silence followed, the congregation waiting for another word. "You are at liberty to go. Please come back next Sunday morning at the same time."

Many shook his hand before they left the building. Some talked among themselves. Mary came up to him when he stood alone.

"My parents said I could invite you to have dinner with us. We are having a picnic out under the trees before we go home." She said.

"Of course, I would be delighted. I just have to gather up the song books." The preacher told her.

"May I help you do that?" She asked.

"Yes. You may." He said with a smile.

When the two got to the shade trees, the dinner was spread already. The people waited for the preacher. He looked a little sheepish at them when they all turned to watch him and the young Mary walk toward them. Mary walked to where her parents were waiting. She exchanged a small smile with her mother. Mister Wilmington gave a stern look which Mary saw through easily. He spoke to the preacher.

"Would you pray for us Brother Newton?" He said.

So there under the trees, a new beginning was established for the young preacher and the new church. He bonded easily with his fellow Christians. He talked of his plans as he ate the dinner. Mary, the cook, had provided fresh fried chicken to go with the vegetables the people brought with them. Mrs. Wilmington came out with a banana pudding made up in a large aluminum dishpan. The icing was slightly browned on top.

"We will just have to build us a church." Mister Wilmington told Brother Newton loud enough for those around him to hear.

"Wouldn' be no different than a barn raising 'cept for the floor." A brawny man said around a leg of chicken.

"I got a sawmill. We can all donate a tree or two." Another man volunteered.

Brother Newton was overcome and sat silently. Mary watched his face and spotted a tear in the corner of one eye. The talk went through the trees like a breeze. Discussions were carried on about how the work could be done and when they could get the work done around the harvesting. One man walked shyly across the shaded area to where the preacher was eating. He wore overalls and work boots. His hair was scarce on top when he removed his hat to talk to the preacher.

"My property runs right out to the road north of town." He said with his head bowed as if to pray. "There is a hill there that would make a fine spot for your church. I would be proud if you would take two acres as a gift. The only charge is that me and my family be buried there when the Lord calls us." He said.

Brother Newton rose to his feet. He extended his hand to the man, after wiping off the chicken grease. The handshake lasted a long time, for a handshake. A stream of unspoken words passed between the two men. Brother Newton reached an arm around the man's shoulder. His name was John Clarity.

"Thank you John." The preacher said.

"You just keep preaching like you done today. We need to be reminded." John said.

John walked back to his family. His wife stood to hug her husband. Then he awkwardly resumed his seat on the grass and reached for his bowl of banana pudding.

Word spread quickly the next week. A new church was being built outside of town on the north end. John Clarity had donated the hill next to the road for the building. The local undertaker knew the first thing they would need after clearing off the land was some foundation rocks. He quietly acquired some granite from his suppliers and dropped them off without a word. The saw-miller worked every evening sawing up logs hauled and dragged to his mill. A few from this farmer and that. James Inkle came out of the mountains with some logs on his old truck. The saw-miller knew what James did for a living and looked up at him a little curious.

"I reckon I can believe in God and make a little moonshine." He said.

"Those logs will make good lumber James." The saw-miller said.

"Listen." James started. "I want to surprise the preacher. I got me a few tools and I would like to make some pews for the new church. Would you saw me up some lumber to do the job?" James asked.

"Sure James. I will use the narrow edges, so we don't waste any of the Lords trees." The miller said.

"I will bring down another load and pick up the lumber next week." James told him.

The miller took off his cap and scratched his head with it, as he watched the moonshiner drive away.

"Now, if that don't beat all." He mumbled as another tree meet the big saw and all other sound was drowned out.

Back at the hotel, Miss Alice was having a good day. She lay on her bed and clapped her hands and sang hymn after hymn. She kept her singing low as best she could but today she was filled with joy. She heard about the new church being built. Doctor Hill went in to check on her.

"You seem happy today." The doctor said.

"My cup runneth over." She said.

"And to what do we credit such joy?" He asked.

"Why, it's the Lord. All good things come from Him." She said.

"Is there any particular good thing that you refer to?" He asked.

"The new church is what makes me so happy." She said.

"We already have a church in town and one on the west side of the county. Do we really need another one?" The doctor asked.

"Of course we do, Will. There is a passel of people up there in the north end. It will be their church, not just one they can visit now and then." She explained.

"That makes a lot of sense. If they build it, they are more likely to attend." The doctor reasoned.

"The Lord knows what he is doing." She said.

The doctor patted her shoulder and went to the kitchen for a fresh cup of coffee. He did not understand her joy. She probably would not be able to attend very many services, yet she was as happy as if she had thought of the idea.

In truth, Miss Alice had thought of it. She had prayed many days and nights away, for a revival to come to the county. She prayed for a young preacher filled with love for the people and the Lords work to come to town. She prayed for a place where the common folks of the county could find the Lord even in their ragged clothes and work shoes.

Week after week, all over the north end of the county, people used every spare minute of their time to work on the church building. There were multi-talented people on the farms. By necessity they were builders as well as farmers. The

43

preacher gave them a rough sketch of the building he envisioned. The men pulled their lines and set the foundation rocks in place. Huge logs were squared to lay on top of the rocks. A sub-floor of rough lumber was put in place. The walls were framed up on the ground and pulled into place with ropes.

Tommy Bookmark found the experience exciting. He did any task assigned to him. He kept his notebook handy to take down the events of the church building project. The ladies all planned their days so extra food could be prepared for whoever was working at the church. People just showed up and did what needed to be done. Brother Newton was there about all the time. He was able to pass messages from one worker to the next, as well as, do some work while the others cared for their crops. Someone got them started making shingles. It seemed a job that would never end. One by one they split the flat pieces of wood from logs sawed into short pieces. Tommy became quiet expert at the task. He knew he got the job because of his lack of skill with the carpentry work but he did not mind. He would learn.

Money from the offerings was enough to purchase tongue-and-groove boards for the floor. They put coat upon coat of finish on the floor to bring the wood to a high gloss. James Inkle showed up about the time the floor dried for the last time. He had a load of pews. Little James stood beside his Pa in new shoes and a smile on his face as big as a hubcap. He had helped with the building of the pews. Brother Newton was surprised when the pews were delivered by Mister Inkle and his son. Apparently, the preacher was the only one who did not know about the pew project. Every time he mentioned pews to anyone, they just put him off.

"The Lord will provide." Someone said.

What could the pastor say to that except to agree.

"I am working on the rest of them, Preacher. We will have them down here by the next service." Mister Inkle told him.

Brother Newton shook hands with the moonshiner. After

all, Jesus did come to call not the righteous but sinners to repentance. Mister Inkle just shrugged the whole thing off.

"We had some time while the mash was curing out." He said honestly.

"I hope you will be here for our first service in the new building." Brother Newton said.

"We will all be here, if the baby ain't sick." Inkle said.

"We will just pray that the baby does not get sick." Brother Newton said.

The people all went their separate ways. It was time for a late supper and to get to bed. Some would have to draw water for a bath. Others would get bath water from rain barrels set under the leak of the house for that purpose. The rain water was also used for washing clothes when the well got low. Tommy decided to stop by the creek and take a plunge by lantern light. It would be cold but quicker than waiting for the tub. The preacher stayed at the church to look over their progress and to pray.

Chapter

6

"Sheriff, we need to talk." Ben Smith was standing in the jail in front of the sheriff. He reached in his pocket and pulled out the federal badge that identified him as a revenue agent for the United States government.

"I guess we do." Sheriff Singletree said.

"I have been watching you Sheriff. You have your finger on the pulse of your county. I doubt if anything happens here that you do not know about. You put people in jail and all they talk about is the good food here." Ben told him.

"It is an elected office." The sheriff said.

"No one can fault you for getting the votes. I believe also that you are an honest man. Practical but honest. Which brings me to my reason for coming to you. Normally, I work alone until there are arrest to be made but your county is different. Your economy is based on three things: farming, logging and moonshine. You know the federal government will go for about anything, so long as they can tax it. Moonshine presents a problem. There is no factory for the inspectors to go to. Moonshiners do not order tax stamps for their jars. So, the government wants to stop them." Agent Smith paused to let that soak in.

"How do you feel about the moonshine?" Sheriff Singletree asked.

"I have a job to do. My job, now, is to keep organized

crime from taking control of the moonshine business. When the moonshine leaves the county, it becomes a state problem. When it leaves the state, it becomes a federal problem. Of course, not having a federal tax stamp makes it a federal problem too." Agent Smith said.

"Listen, before you get me mad and upset my appetite, let's have a bite to eat. Sarah has it ready, if my nose is not deceiving me." Sheriff Singletree said.

"Are you sure?" Agent Smith asked.

"Sure, I'm sure. We can eat first and give each other 'what for' later." The sheriff said.

"The people in the city could take lessons from you folks. You are smarter than you let on." Agent Smith said.

"We are as smart as we have to be." The sheriff said.

"When in Rome....." Agent Smith let the quote trail off.

"...do as the Romans do." The sheriff finished for him.

Agent Smith laughed out loud. He realized that there was more to the sheriff than a big bellied, slap-you-on-the-back hillbilly. He was playing a part. There was no point in using fancy words with people who did not know what they meant. The sheriff had learned to deal with his county in the country, laid-back manner in which they were accustomed. He was one of them. He would shot a man, as a criminal, but weep over him as his friend. People here had a strange code he could never be privy to, but he understood it. The nation was united in the greater sense but each facet of the country had its own code, its own language. The street thugs lived by their code. The crime bosses had theirs. Even within law enforcement, there was a code. They would never think of ratting on a fellow cop but would cuff a citizen for breaking the same law.

"We live in a strange world." Smith said it aloud without realizing.

"You are right about that." The sheriff said.

"What?" Agent Smith asked.

"You were thinking out loud. Yes. It is a strange world. Your food is getting cold. I thought we had lost you there for a minute. Sarah already prayed, so dig in." Sheriff Singletree told him.

They sat on the porch now, watching the traffic go by. A strange mixture of mules, horses, trucks and cars. It seemed as if two lines in time were trying to crisscross each other right here in Hatsworth. Indeed, such was the case. Both men pondered the street in front of them.

"Now, what is this about organized crime? Why are they interested in our little county?" Sheriff Singletree asked.

"Not just your county. They have people in the counties from here to North Carolina and beyond. There is a big market for moonshine in the cities and they want to be the middle man. They have cars that will outrun ours. Sometimes, I think they are better organized than our agency but we are trying." Agent Smith said.

"So, what brings you here at this particular time?" The sheriff asked him.

"A smart-mouthed young man named Lawrence Aulding. He is a front man for organized crime. He has large ambitions but right now his mission is this county. He is buying rights to ninety percent of the whiskey that is made here. At least, that is their usual percentage. They leave ten percent for the locals, as they call you." Agent Smith explained.

"The moonshiners do pay taxes in a round about way. They spend all their money here and must pay taxes when they spend it." The sheriff reasoned. "So, they call us locals, do they?"

"Yep." Agent Smith answered.

"I guess they mean something by that but I ain't figured out what yet. If I find out it is an insult, they will deal with me." The sheriff said.

"What's the plan? The sheriff added.

"Simple. I have to catch Aulding with a load of whiskey. We will put him away for a few years. The crime bosses will try again with someone else but catching Aulding will set them back for a while." Agent Smith said.

"Okay. Let's catch him." Sheriff Singletree said.

Aulding had taken another man with him on his trips to pickup the moonshine. It would be that man's job to make the pickups after he learned the route. Tonight was the other man's first run with a load. Aulding waited at strategic points along the route to make sure everything was going according to plan. It was a mistake by Agent Smith that he did not know of the second car. The two cars came out of the mountains to the main road and headed south. Aulding was bringing up the rear. He was riding very close to the other car. It would appear to an onlooker that he wanted to pass.

The sheriff and Agent Smith fell in behind the two cars. Their hope was that the other car would turn off someplace and leave the road to Aulding and the two officers. The sheriff drove his county car while Smith drove his unmarked vehicle. The whiskey runners gained speed as they left town. If the sheriff could have seen the tag on the lead car, he would have known it was from the same area as Aulding. On a straight-a-way south of town, Aulding pulled out to pass the other car. Sheriff Singletree noticed the tag then, but accelerated to pass so he could get behind Aulding. There was no posted speed limit on the open road. Aulding pushed the accelerator down on the big car. It put some distance between him and the sheriff. The sheriff's car was not equipped for high-speed chases. Agent Smith's car was a different story. He pushed his accelerator to the floor and overtook the sheriff, then passed him. He caught up with Aulding and passed him, waving as he went around. He wanted to appear to be a young man just out for a good road race. Once he got in front of Aulding, he slowed his pass as if teasing the man.

Aulding pulled over to pass Agent Smith. Smith blocked him and slowed down even more. The sheriff was catching up. There was a hill up ahead. Smith slowed down more causing Aulding to downshift. He moved to the right to try to pass. Smith blocked once more. Meanwhile, Sheriff Singletree pulled up in the left lane beside Aulding and motioned for him to move to the side of the road. The sheriff was angry. He climbed out of his car pulling his pistol belt back up to where his waist ought to be. Agent Smith pulled off at a distance so he could watch the action. The other car that Aulding was running with came by them at a slow pace. He acted like a curious motorist.

The sheriff invited Aulding to step out of the car. He looked under the seats and in the trunk. There was no whiskey.

"Don't you stop when the law tells you to?" The sheriff asked.

"Yes sir. I thought you were after someone else." Aulding said.

"I was after you. You need to come through town slower. We have pedestrians and horses in the streets." He said.

"I am sorry Sheriff. I will slow down. What about that guy up there? He was blocking the road." Aulding complained.

"I am just about to speak to him. You can go now. Be more careful." Singletree scolded.

The sheriff pulled up behind Agent Smith. Aulding passed them at a slow speed as he went through the gears. He smiled and waved at the two.

"What happened?" Sheriff Singletree asked after he had passed.

"They must have had two cars. My money is on the one he followed out of town." Agent Smith said.

"I noticed it had an out-of-town tag but I was so mad at Aulding, all I wanted to do was get around him. It did not look like it had a load." The sheriff observed.

"They put truck springs under them, so they don't sit down in the back. He would look funny empty but once he gets a load the car sits just about right." Agent Smith said.

Aulding made immediate changes when he got to the city. From now on there would be one man to haul the whiskey and another to run interference. He planned and supervised the car modifications himself. He wanted a powerful motor and a transmission that would allow for higher top-end speeds. He also had them install toggle switches for the lights. When the switch was flipped, the taillights would be dark even with the driver's foot on the brakes. He brought in a driver from out of state to run the interference car. The man had been racing on dirt tracks for several years. He also found out that there was a revenue agent working in his county. A secretary in the department provided that information. All he had to do was buy her dinner and pretend to be attracted to her. She was not all that bad looking anyway. Aulding had no inclination to fall in love. She was just a tool of the business. So much the better, if she was a looker. Now, he was ready for the next run. He had a little surprise for Agent Smith.

Chapter

7

Tommy Bookmark picked cotton as if he were born to it.
He took Mister McNeil's example and straddled one row
while picking the row on either side. He took to carrying an
extra picksack so he could fill two without having to stop to
weigh up. Finally, all the cotton was picked and sent to the
gin. For the first time since he went to work there, they took a
Saturday off. In celebration of getting the cotton picked
before it rained, they had a watermelon cutting. All the hands
were invited to the McNeil home. Of course, they could not
have watermelon only. There was a lot of fixings including:
apple pies and roasted corn.

Tommy walked with Marsha to a green hill in the pasture.
A branch of the creek ran around the base of the hill. They
looked out over the fields. The cotton fields were a dark
brown color now with a shade of green. He learned that some
boles would open late, perhaps not to full bloom, but still
worth picking. The technique used for the last picking was to
strip the cotton off bole and all. The product did not pay as
much as clean cotton but would still provide some income and
not waste anything. There was no room for waste on a farm.

The corn was now tasseled and the blades turning brown.
In just a few days, it would be time to 'pull' the ears and stow

them in the crib. They would take some to be ground whole for feed and some would be shucked, shelled and taken to the grist meal. All along, the garden was 'coming in' and produce was being picked for canning.

He had learned a lot. His notebook was full but not as full as his heart. He had learned to love everything about farm life. He saw it as a cycle. The farmers job was to work within the cycle and reap the rewards for his sweat. Tommy loved the smell of the dirt. He loved the mixture of odors that passed in the breeze. The summer was passing very fast. His stay at the farm had gone from a learning experience to a heartfelt attachment and love for the rigorous, simple life. More than all these feelings, he had fallen in love with the farmers daughter.

Marsha stood beside him on the hill. The breeze lifted her hair and let it fall back to her shoulders. She gazed up at him as he looked at the fields and was lost in thought.

"Where did you go?" She asked.

"I was right here." He said.

"Your eyes looked so distant." She said.

"I was thinking about the last couple of months. Marsha, I have a good education. My desire has been to write about the world around me. To experience it, then put it on paper." He said.

"And now?" She questioned.

"My desires have changed dramatically. I still want to write but I could find peace here on this farm. I have found peace here." He corrected himself. "Soon the summer will be over, I do not want to leave. I have fallen in love with you."

"I have also fallen in love with you, Tommy Bookmark." She said softly.

"The world will change soon. Our perfect time in history will be shattered. Let's get married, now, while things are so good. We can go through the hard times together." He said.

"Yes." She said.

"What?" He asked.

"I said yes, Mister Bookmark. You did just ask me to marry you, didn't you?" She said pretending to pout.

"Yes. Yes I did. You will?" He took her in his arms and kissed her for the first time.

Back at the house, Mister McNeil and his wife stood on the porch. He braced his hands on the cross-member of the porch. She wrapped one arm around his waist.

"We should not let them see us watching them." She said.

"He is kissing our daughter. I've a good mind to..." He started.

"She is a grown woman. She has worked all her life without the first complaint. Marsha is a sensible girl. She would not let a man kiss her if she was not in love with him." Mrs. McNeil said.

"I suppose. Well, we should have some of that coffee before it gets bitter." They turned as one toward the kitchen.

They drank their coffee and waited for the announcement that Bill had dreaded longer than he needed to. Tommy and Marsha made a long walk of returning to the house. Bill finally busied himself with the evening chores. Darkness was falling when the couple returned to the house. Mrs. McNeil was working on her embroidery while Bill worked his way through the book of Proverbs.

"Mister McNeil, I need to ask you something." Tommy said.

Mrs. McNeil rose to her feet. "Marsha and I will go look at the stars for a while." She said.

Tommy made a short story long. He told Mister McNeil about all the plans he had made for his life. He reiterated his reasons for coming to the farm. They were the same as he had told him on the first day. Then, he told him how the life of a farmer had captured his heart. At long last, he told of his love for Marsha and asked if he would give them his blessings.

"I thought you would never get to that part. I reckon this farm is too big for one man to look after. I got a hundred acres that needs to be seeded next year. The pasture can stand another fifty head of cattle. We have enough timber back up against the mountain to build you a house. My daughter could not do better than you." Bill caught a breath. That was the longest speech he had ever made.

Tommy started to run out through the kitchen to tell Marsha then turned around to shake hands with Mister McNeil.

"Thank you. Thank you, sir. I will look after her with my life." Tommy assured him. Then he was out the door. He grabbed Marsha and swung her around and around.

"You two ain't married yet." Bill said gruffly from the kitchen door. Tommy let her drop to the ground gently. Then long after the McNeil's had gone to bed, they sat under the starry sky and talked of their plans for the future. Tomorrow after church, they would pick out a spot for their house. The hill they stood on today might be a good place. As soon as he could get to town, he would go to the bank and send for his savings. He would pick up a catalog so Marsha could shop for curtains, silverware and such.

Tomorrow would be a good day. Tommy felt that all the rest of his days could be nothing but good.

The preacher was on new floors. The congregation was on new pews. They were all in a new building but the preacher did not deliver a feel-good message. He preached himself out of his coat and tie. Sweat drenched his shirt. He marched them all up to the door of hell then snatched them away by the grace of God. The smell of new varnish gave way to the smell of burning sulphur. The altar filled when the invitation was given. The sound was one of people pleading as they slipped down a slop toward the lake of fire. Then one of joy, as one by one the hand of mercy lifted them out of harms way. After the service, they all went down to the creek and baptized the new converts. The sun was hot in the afternoon and the clothes soon dried as dinner was spread on the ground. It was a glorious time when people answered the call of God with open hearts and God welcomed them with open arms.

James Inkle sat on the grass with his family. He recalled the morning service vividly. He came to the service to please his wife. Their children needed to know about God, she had told him. Little James sat on the other side of Mrs. Inkle. At first, James was admiring the new pews he had made. He knew every piece of wood. He remembered the trees as they stood before he sawed them down for lumber. The preacher was in the last portion of his sermon when James realized that the message was for him. He had lived a pretty good life. The moonshine he made was of top quality and had never made anyone sick. He did not hit his wife and would have thought the idea absurd. There was something missing in his life. He had never considered that the Son of God would find it necessary to die for his sins. Oh, he knew he had sins but he had tried to be a good husband and parent. Mrs. Inkle had talked about when she used to go to church and even when she went to the altar as a young girl. She was feeding the baby now to keep her quiet during the sermon.

James felt his hands tremble and held onto his knees to steady them. He envisioned himself standing before God while his life was played back to him. He had no defense. God was right and he deserved what ever punishment was handed out. Then the preacher told of a way to escape the awful punishment. James knew a good deal when he saw one. By the time the invitation was given, his knuckles had turned white from gripping his knees so hard. He took several long strides and was bowing before a Holy God. He knew when the love of Jesus encompassed his soul. He knew when he was snatched from the jaws of hell. He stood unashamed before the congregation and told his story. While he was testifying, his son walked down the aisle and bowed in the altar. He too received forgiveness and eternal life. Mrs. Inkle had stopped feeding the baby. She was bouncing happily on her mother's hip as Mrs. Inkle rejoiced between the pews her husband had made.

Tommy was among the others who bowed that day for forgiveness. He had never made moonshine or lived a wild life. He had always assumed that his good life would win favor with God when the time came. Then, he saw the sinful nature of mankind as the story was told of Adam's sin and the hopeless efforts of mankind to redeem himself. He realized that there was nothing within himself that could justify him before a Holy God. He wondered at the sacrifice made by God in giving His Son for a mere man, such as himself. He had committed the greater sin by ignoring the great sacrifice of love made for him. Marsha stood beside him as he told his story, her face wet with tears. She had rededicated her life to the making of a Christian home.

Old-fashioned people in an old-fashioned way met the Lord that day on His terms. He honored their commitment with joy in their hearts. They came to understand the simplicity of salvation in a world that was becoming much too complicated.

Tommy felt such love for Marsha that his words became inadequate to describe how he felt. He knew that this must be the greatest love of all. Then, he met the Lord. The thought that he would live forever was overwhelming. The relief of having his burden of sin removed amazed him. His sharp intellect could not figure it out. He could not understand why a God he had never met would love him so much. Yet He did. He understood why the song *Amazing Grace* (by John Newton) was so dear to Christians. It was their only way to express the blessings poured out upon them without measure. Later, he would read the passage about loving his wife as

Christ loved the church and gave Himself for it, some grasp of His love would sink in. For now, he was just happy that he was included in the plan.

With so many new Christians in the congregation, even the blessing at meal time became a reason for rejoicing. It seemed that all the words held special meaning for them. Mrs. Inkle rejoiced over her new family. She knew things would be a lot different around her house. She had not mentioned the moonshine making to her husband and knew that it would not be necessary. God would show him what to do. No doubt, it was on James' mind even now. She prayed for him as he faced the difficult decisions ahead.

James got up to talk to the preacher. He had made his decision. Moonshine did not fit in with his new life. He was concerned about how to make a living for his family. The preacher got everyone's attention and made the announcement. James was no longer going to make moonshine. The preacher asked everyone to pray about a way for James to make a living for his family. It was the Christian way to share burdens. James went back to his place. Mrs. Inkle patted his shoulder. The baby reached for him and he took the child in his arms. He received a hug he desperately needed.

As the meal time neared an end, people began to walk by where James and his family were finishing up.

"I need a cabinet for the kitchen. Would you build it for me?" One woman asked.

"Yes ma'am. Just write down your name and what you need." James told her.

"I need a seed room built in my barn. Could you do it for me? I have so much work that I cannot get around to it." A man said.

"My well shed is about to rot out. Could you redo it for me?" Another asked.

Before the afternoon was over, James had enough work to keep him and his son busy for the winter. Tommy took note of all the things going on. He was witnessing the workings of God first-hand. How could he ever put all this to paper?

The meeting broke up and the congregation went to their separate homes. Tommy and Marsha walked to the hill where they had decided to give each other their lives. They decided that the hill would be a good place to raise their family. A hill on the other end of the property had been considered but they decided to build close to her parents. It was senseless to have to go all the way across the property. There would be grandchildren who would visit their grandparents often. Marsha and her mother would need to spend time together, talking, canning and preparing meals. Living on the other side of the property was just not practical. There would be days ahead when this decision would seem even more right. They discussed where to put the various rooms of the house. They decided on an upstairs built into the attic for the day when they were blessed with children. The master bedroom would be downstairs. A kitchen, dining room and living room finished their plans. Tommy had plans to bring water into the house. He knew about a pump that was being used to draw well-water. He had enough savings to get the wood sawed. Mister McNeil had already offered to provide the trees.

James Inkle went home and walked to his woodshed to retrieve his ax. He walked back in the woods where a spring bubbled up out of the ground. It was also where his still was located. He swung the ax with mighty blows as he cut into the copper pot of the still. He poured the whisky into an old rotted-out stump hole to keep it from running into the stream. He came back into the house with sweat running off his face. A big smile broke out on his face as his wife and son looked at him.

"I have to get rid of temptation." He said.

"You did the right thing." His wife said.

"What do you think Mister Aulding is going to say now?" Little James asked.

"I expect he will be upset but we will explain it to him."

James told him.

Brother Paul Newton sat in the front of the church on the first pew. He breathed a silent prayer of thanks to God for all the days events. It was what he had hoped for but more than he expected. The people seemed to be bonded together already. He walked around the pews straightening the song books and praying for those who would occupy the pews. He wondered at what might be ahead for the community. Was the Lord preparing them for some dark days? His mind drifted to the newspaper accounts of the war in Europe. Of the rumors of crop destroying weevils. He felt guilt at trying to reason over the blessings of God. Yet, he also knew that sometimes Christians were prepared for hardships with a time of spiritual uplifting.

Oh well, he was here for the good times, he would stay with the people when things got rough. These sheep were in his care.

Chapter
8

Doctor Hill made the announcement at supper. They had
brought Miss Alice down for the evening meal. Sheriff
Singletree was in attendance. He had also brought his wife,
Sarah. The jail was empty, so she did not have to cook for
prisoners. Brother Newton was there, as was Mister Aulding.
Mister Aulding was ignorant that he was under suspicion of
running moonshine for organized crime. The Revenue Agent,
Mister Smith, was enjoying the delicious meal. The hotel
dining area had become a, so-called, neutral ground. Marsha
and Mary Wilmington served the food and kept the glasses
filled, or coffee cups in some cases.
   "Ladies and Gentlemen, I have an announcement to make.
The evening newspaper just came in and it contains a very
important announcement." Doctor Hill began. "The
President has announced that the United States will be
entering the war in Europe. The selective service has already
sent notices out to those who will serve in the war." He said.
   A silence ensued around the table. They waited. Then the
doctor read the full article to the group. Everyone knew that
they would all be affected by this announcement.
   The people got up from their places and quietly left the
hotel. Word of the story spread rapidly in the county. People

stopped by houses on their way home to tell their neighbors. The preacher went out to tell the McNeil's and the Clarity's. By the end of the week, those who had been selected had received their notices. Marsha wept as Tommy showed her his unopened envelope. When they finally did open it, he found out that he was to leave in two weeks for his assigned unit. He received a commission as a lieutenant in the United States Army.

Little James received his notice and was to report to the same unit as Tommy.

"Let's get married before you leave. We have two weeks and I want us to be together every minute." Marsha said.

"I would like that but what if something happens?" Tommy asked.

"Then, I will have my memories but I believe you will return to me. You have things to do after the war." She said.

"Okay. It is settled. We will get married right away and I will hurry back home from the war." He said.

Tommy talked to Brother Newton and made the arrangements for the following Sunday after the morning worship.

Sunday morning was a somber time at church. Many families had someone who was leaving by the end of the next week. They all knew that some would not return. He preached on heaven and the wonderful hope all Christians have in life after death. He told them that the church would be in constant prayer for their safe return. And so the men departed.

Lieutenant Bookmark marched his troops the remaining half mile to the trenches. Their trip involved a series of modes of transportation. Many of his troops got sick on the transatlantic ship ride. Tommy, however, enjoyed the trip. The sunsets were the best. He was always amazed at their beauty. They were on blackout at night. German U-boats were reported to be lurking in the waters. The feared U-boats could run at fifteen knots for two hours under water. They possessed advanced underwater listening equipment and six forward torpedo tubes. It was recommended that the troops walk softly and above all not to drop anything. There was no smoking on deck. It was so dark at times that someone could be standing three feet away without Tommy knowing it until they coughed or something. Needless to say, to fall overboard was a death sentence. There would be no rescue effort with the Germans watching and listening for them.

World War I was basically trench warfare until introduction of the tanks. On the Western Front "armies of millions of men faced each other in a line of trenches extending from the Belgian coast through northeastern France to Switzerland."*

*Britannica

The trenches were dug in a zigzag manner to prevent a straight line of fire from the end. Machine guns were used primarily in the forward trenches. Further back the main body was dug-in using a series of trenches with supplies and command post. There were dugouts for troops during bombardments. The assaults were preceded with artillery shelling. The element of surprise was thus lost because the artillery acted as a warning to the enemy that an attack was imminent. It also torn up the battlefield leaving holes which were difficult for the troops to cross rapidly. Some of Germany's trenches were as much as fourteen miles long.

Into this madness, Lieutenant Bookmark marched his men. The last part of their trip was through the series of trenches to the command post. They passed mud clad soldiers. Some slept, an exhausted sleep, against the walls of the trenches. Others were trying to write letters on crumpled paper. Others stared at them as they went by in their clean uniforms. Some of his men greeted the veteran soldiers and received only grunts in return.

They passed a dugout with a red cross over the door. A man walked out ducking his head. He had a white bandage around his forehead. He adjusted his helmet as he walked so it would fit over the bandages. Men were on stretchers inside the dugout. Tommy wondered where they found white sheets in this mud hole. Finally, they came to the command post of the battalion they were assigned to. He gave his men leave to rest and smoke if they desired. He took his platoon sergeant with him into command headquarters.

The battalion commander was not much older than Tommy but the lines in his face made him look much older. He greeted Tommy with a wide smile.

"Our job is to hold this cornfield or advance to the cow pasture, if so ordered." He said, using the original purpose of the battlefield.

"The world would be better off if it was still a cornfield. Sir." Lieutenant Bookmark said boldly.

"I agree." The commander said. "Since we are here, we just as well keep it from the Germans." The commander took no offense.

"Will I be able to keep my unit together?" Tommy asked.

"Not a chance. It would be suicide for you and them. They will be used to fill vacancies in other units so they can be with veterans. You will keep two squads of your men. You may pick them. The outpost units are due for rotation. You will command and defend our machine gun placements." He said.

"Yes sir. When do we move out?" Lieutenant Bookmark asked.

"You have thirty minutes." He said. "By-the-way, my name is Hank Stanza. I am from New York. Call me Hank unless I am mad. Then you can call me Lieutenant Colonel Stanza."

"Yes sir." Tommy said. They exchanged a grime smile as Tommy turned to instruct his troops. He was given a map of the trenches which he was to guard with his very life. In enemy hands, the map would mean the death of countless men.

Tommy picked two squads. He took James Inkle with him, two sergeants picked the balance of his command. His men would replace two squads on the front-line trench. Two squads of veterans would remain on the front to bring his platoon back to strength. The rotating commander would take two squads back to the rear trenches.

It was a little deceiving to refer to the trenches as forward and rear. All were in reach of the deadly artillery. The front trenches were the most dangerous place to be, as they would be hit first and the hardest in the case of the inevitable attack. They were to man the machine guns until told to retreat through the trenches to the main body. That order may or may not be given depending on the wishes of the brass.

Tommy stopped his men before they arrived.

"Keep you head down. Do not be looking over the top unless told to do so. You can sightsee after the war is over. You will be spread out throughout the platoon so that you will be with a veteran of this mess. If they give good advice, take it. If they tell you to do something stupid, use your head. That is it." He concluded.

He halted them inside the trench they were to defend. The men already there were rotated on the same basis. Those going to the rear were ready for their departure. A staff sergeant came to him immediately.

"Sir, I am due for rotation but I would like to stay with my men." He said.

"I would be glad to have you if it is okay with your commanding officer." Lieutenant Bookmark said.

"He said it was fine with him. He did not recommend it but did say I could stay." The sergeant's commanding officer was standing nearby and gave Tommy a slight nod.

"Very well, Sergeant. Distribute my men as you see fit. I want them with your men so they can learn to stay alive." He

said.

"That is why I am staying, Sir, I will see to it."

"What's your name Sergeant?" Tommy asked.

"Patrick Sparks, Sir. Everybody calls me Sparky." He replied.

"You can call me Tommy unless I am mad, then you can call me Lieutenant Bookmark or Sir." Tommy said.

The rotating commanding officer walked up to Tommy when the sergeant had left on his business.

"You will do alright Tommy. You just made the best friend you can have up here in this ditch." He said.

"What's the deal here?" Tommy asked.

"Hold the ditch." He said.

"Any advice?" Tommy asked.

"Keep a check on the weapons. If you get attacked, there will be no time to do it then. The men tend to get sloppy after a few days with nothing to do." He said.

"Thanks Captain, have a nice vacation at the rear." Tommy said.

"Yeah, right." He said as he followed his anxious troops through the trenches.

Lieutenant Bookmark went first to his machine gun placements. He checked the weapons and ammunition supply. He then walked the line to let the men see him. Next, he order the sergeant to have every other man strip his weapon and clean it. Then repeated the order with the other men. The men mumbled but settled down soon, seemingly happy to have something to do. He got on the communication line (comm) with battalion and ordered more ammo. He ordered the men to dig a hole in the back of the trench to store the additional ammunition until needed. He had no intention of getting killed because they ran out of bullets. He reinforced the machine gun placements with marksmen, who looked through a hole below the machine gunner. Their job was to defend the gunner. If he lost the machine guns, he would loss his men. He also had the men dig safe zones into the trenches so they could drop a curtain and smoke or take a nap in rotation. Thus preventing the temptation to light up and give away their position for a sniper. He also designated snipers of his own to watch for a careless enemy. It was a bit of a low-down tactic but one less enemy increased their chances for survival. That night he asked for volunteers to crawl out a few feet to place booby traps, hand grenades with pull strings, to help if they were overrun. They were now as ready as he could make them. He keep James by his side as his aid and runner. He wanted someone he could trust to get the message straight.

He settled back with a can of peaches and wrote his first letter home.

My Darling Marsha,

This letter will be short. I am now with my troops on the front line. I hesitated to tell you as much, but we have promised to be honest with each other. We have prepared as well as we can. Killing is not my life's ambition but this war must be ended and the enemy defeated. I already want to come home. The burden of command is great with these men hanging on my every word. All my words are meant to help them live to get home. I am sorry, I could not help get the corn in. I know it will be hard on you and your folks. Just wanted to let you know I made the trip okay. The sunsets were beautiful on the open sea. Lots of love.

Tommy

Tommy pulled a little trickery on the Germans across the field on his first night. He put his marksmen in place and told them to watch for muzzle flashes. Then he lit the end of a stick and held it up for the Germans to see. The stick drew fire from the enemy. He held up another stick and drew more fire. His marksmen had found their target with the first burst of gun fire. When the enemy fired the second time, his marksmen shot at the flashes. The action served two purposes. It eliminated some of the enemy and it would make them think twice before shooting at any of his men who forgot to conceal their lights. The Germans got mad and cut loose with a barrage of machine gun fire but Tommy had already told his men to hunker down. As the machine guns fired, his marksmen, peeping through their small holes between the sandbags, found other targets to shot at. The Germans, finally, stopped falling for the trickery and settled down for the night. Tommy put his men on rotating naps and took one himself, leaving the sergeant in charge.

"You got all the men wanting to take a crack at the peepholes." Sparky told Lieutenant Bookmark.

"Well, if you know of a good marksman, he will get his chance. But not tonight. We will let them wonder what we are up to." He said.

Sparky laughed as he went off on his rounds. The man seemed to be in constant motion. Sometimes he would stop to talk to one of the troops and casually check his weapon as he talked. The men expected it and were not offended. They even felt more secure after the sergeant had given his approval on the condition of the rifle. He counted ammunition from habit. He told the men to watch the pull strings on the grenades.

"Let's don't give away our little secret by setting off a grenade. We may need them if they get in close." He told them over and over.

The third night Tommy lit his stick and held it up. An anxious German was killed after his second shot at the stick. On the fourth night, the Germans came. There was no moon. Tommy's men could not see each other except as vague shadows. Tommy was checking posts when one of the marksmen whispered to him.

"Sir, it may not be anything but I saw the barbed wire move a while ago. I would not have noticed it but my eyes are pretty good in the dark. The wire jerked a couple of times like when you have a fish nibbling on bait." The soldier said.

"Good job." Tommy turned to James who was on his heels. "Run as fast and as quiet as you can down the line. Tell them the Germans are coming under the wire without their usual artillery show. Tell them it is time to look over the wall and be ready. Go."

James ran the line telling the squad leaders the orders. The troops plastered themselves to the wall of the trench, looking over just enough to see any close movement. Tommy looked through the peephole. He stared for a few minutes and saw the wire move again. He heard someone curse in a whisper at the man who had gotten hung on the wire. The curse was in German. He slapped the machine gunner on the leg.

"Spray the entire field. Let them know we see them." Tommy said. He ran down the line to his position and looked carefully over the wall. There was not much to see. Just in case, he pulled a string on one of the grenade booby traps. A man screamed and they all knew the Germans were right on top of them.

"Fire at will." He yelled. The command was passed down the line. The strings were pulled and followed by a stream of rifle fire. The Germans could not rise to charge because they were under the barb wire. The dead men killed by the grenades blocked their way. All they could do was stay in place and fire their weapons. Each time they fired, they became a target for the machine gunners. The battle was over in thirty minutes.

A German fell over the wall. He had been wounded by the grenade. He begged for them not to kill him. They took him prisoner. Back at the command post, he was questioned using an interpreter. He told how his commander had become outraged at the trickery of the American commander. His German commander ordered an attack to teach him a lesson.

Hank laughed as he heard the story. He called Tommy on the comm and told him congratulations and to keep doing what ever he was doing to make the Germans act irrationally.

A week went by with both sides sniping at each other. Then, artillery shells started coming from behind the German lines. They sailed over the heads of Tommy's position. The word came that the barrage was going on all down the Allied lines. It could mean only one thing, a major assault by the Germans was imminent. Tommy walked up and down the line, as Allied artillery answered that of the Germans.

"We have been ordered to hold our position. There will be no withdrawal to the rear." Lieutenant Bookmark told his men.

So, this was it. Someone would win today and someone would lose. The artillery continued in an effort by the Germans to soften up the Allied forces before the ground assault. Tommy was writing a hurried letter to Marsha before the shells started whizzing overheard. He stuffed the letter inside his uniform and waited. A deathly silence had fallen over the battlefield. The soldiers in the rear shook dust from their helmets and uniforms, then checked their weapons.

Then, the Germans came out of their trenches and advanced on the Allied lines. German after German fell but others climbed from the trenches and stepped over their fallen comrades into the blistering fire of the machine guns. Finally, some of them began to make it through the relentless fire. They crawled, ran and stumbled forward, a wave of humanity moving into certain death.

Sparky moved up and down the line, firing where someone had died leaving a hole in their line. All along the line, men fell backward into the trench. Tommy began moving up and down the line as Sparky was doing. His presence seemed to encourage the men.

"Use your grenades!" He yelled.

They pulled the fragmentation devices from their belt and

threw them over the wall of the trench. Then, followed it
with fire from their rifles. The Germans managed to cut the
barbed wire and pull it back. Grenades started to fall into the
trench. His men grabbed them and threw them back at the
Germans.

"Fix bayonets!" He commanded.

Over the wall the Germans came, some jumping into
bayonets, others falling into the trenches after losing their
footing. Finally, when all seemed to be lost, Lieutenant
Colonel Stanza ordered his men, in the rear, out of their
trenches. They came with energy and determination to
defend their fellow soldiers.

Lieutenant Bookmark was fighting hand to hand with a big
German when the man went limp and fell into his arms. He
tossed the body aside. A grenade landed near him and a body
fell across it, absorbing its awful destructive power. There
was no time to see who the man was that had fallen on the
grenade. He left the trench with the battalion and advanced
on the Germans. The offensive attack by Stanza had
surprised the Germans. Their momentum was broken and
they began to fall back. All down the lines, the Allied forces
advanced against the onslaught and pushed them back into
their trenches. Grenade after grenade was tossed in after
them. Then the trenches were taken.

Bodies littered the battlefield, both German and Allied.
Corpsmen were working in the field at a fantastic speed to
check for wounded, to stop bleeding, to stop and listen for
just a moment to a dying man. They helped the fallen men of
Allied forces, then the Germans who were wounded.
Compassion may have seemed strange toward a soldier of the
German army. But these men, some were mere boys, looked
up with grateful eyes toward those who gave them comfort in
their last minutes of life. They, too, had left someone at home
who loved them.

Lieutenant Bookmark walked back to his trench. He
wondered where James was. He always stayed by his side

unless he was on some errand. Tommy looked at the bodies as he worked his way through the carnage but did not spot James anywhere. Then he remembered the grenade that had fallen beside him. He assumed, that by some stroke of providence, a dead body had fallen on the grenade. Now, he feared the worst.

He climbed down into the trench and climbed over bodies to the spot he remembered. He turned the man over who had fallen on the grenade and met the eyes of the man who had saved his life. James' face was strained but he managed a grime smile.

"Tell Maw and Pa that I love them and to not worry about me." James said.

"You can tell them yourself. I will get a corpsman." Tommy told him.

"No. Please stay with me. Do not feel bad for me. I would do the same thing again. You have a purpose in life. Mine was to protect you. I hope I did a good job." James said.

"You did a fine job, James." Tommy said as he held James' head in his arms.

"Tell them...tell them that I will see them again." James said as his head fell against his commanding officer and his friend.

Tommy bent over the young man and wept bitter tears. He rocked him as if to comfort a baby. Lieutenant Colonel Stanza found him later still cradling his friend. The colonel put his hand firmly on the lieutenant's shoulder.

"I am sorry, Tommy, for the loss of your friend." Stanza said.

"Thank you sir. He was a good boy." Tommy said.

"You should let the corpsmen take care of him. Your other men need you, now, more than ever. You are their strength. So wipe away the tears Lieutenant and led them." Stanza said firmly.

"You are right sir." He stood to his feet and straightened his uniform. He looked around for his men.

"They are in the German trench. We made progress toward ending the war today. The cost was great but these men will be honored as long as we have a world to stand on." Stanza told him.

My Darling Marsha,

The Colonel says we made progress in the war today. We fought our way from the cornfield to the cow pasture. I will not describe the battlefield, suffice it to say, that I feel much older than last week.

It has rained for two days, perhaps it is the angels weeping or the Lord cleaning up the blood we spilled on the earth. The trenches are a foot deep in water and everything is mud. I am afraid I lost my razor, so I am a mess.

I received several letters from you today. I have read one of them. I will save the others to read later. Not because I do not want to read them now, but I will need them, then, as well.

There is sad news but I cannot tell it to you until I write another letter and it has time to arrive in the states. You may guess what is the matter but please do not tell anyone.

I am sorry for the bad handwriting but my hands won't stop shaking. It must be a chill from all the rain.

> *I love you so much my heart hurts,*
> *Your husband,*
> *Tommy*

Chapter

9

Little James came home a week after the letter arrived telling of his death. His Medal of Honor was delivered by a colonel from the reserve unit in the capitol. His grave was the first in the cemetery of the new church. An honor guard comprised of various branches of the military services carried his coffin. After the rifle salute, a lone bugler played taps, as he stood alone under one of the big oak trees. Brother Newton took as his text "Home at Last" bringing tears to the eyes of even the battle-hardened colonel.

The citation read at the grave side told of his sacrifice. Marsha recognized her husbands words mixed into the story. Big James draped his big arm around his wife and child. He did not attempt to hide his tears as they fell freely to the front of his suit. His thoughts were of the day he had walked down the aisle and gave his life to the Lord. Then of his son, who had quietly followed his example. He was a boy of simple purpose. He recognized the right thing to do and did it.

Office of the President of the United States

Private First Class James Inkle served as he died with honor and love for his country, his fellow man, and his God. On many occasions, he bravely, with disregard for his own safety, defended his unit and commanding officer. His attention to duty had no equal and displayed the highest standards of America's fighting men. When the moment came for him to make the ultimate sacrifice to save the life of his beloved commander, he did not hesitate to fall on a grenade thus saving his commander's life.

His dying words expressed no regret for his action, his love for his family and the simple words "I would do it again."

We honor him today, with the highest expression of appreciation of a grateful nation, the Medal of Honor.

May we all do as well, for he has not fallen, but rather has risen to a much higher plain.

Signed by The President of the United States

And so, the war touched the small community where nothing seemed out of place before. The people were sobered, as they realized that even events across the ocean could profoundly change their lives. The events were not just a newspaper story. Now, they were very personal. The words of the preacher about a better place to go after this life were more real and meaningful. It was no longer uncommon to hear parents praying in the fields and woods for the soldiers on the battlefield. One man told of a day when he walked home from town and heard his neighbor crying out to God, in the woods beside the road. He predicted "the boys will come home now, people are praying." The small community was no longer an oasis apart from the world. The finger of war and death had reached out to touch them.

Marsha sat down at home, after the funeral, to write Tommy a letter. She told him about the funeral and all the arrangements that had been made giving as much detail as possible. Then, she told Tommy that he was going to be a daddy. She had hesitated to tell him the news for fear it would make him careless in some way. Finally, after considering all the possibilities, she decided that he needed all the hope he could get from home.

Not everyone was sobered by the war. Aulding was still working on his moonshine deliveries. He had gone to Inkle's place to find no moonshine for pickup. He braved the creek and drove up to James' house. Fortunate for him, it was before word came of Little James' death. Mister Inkle patiently told Aulding the story of his conversion although he did not yet now that word. He just told him. "Mister Aulding, I just got saved and I do not think it is right for me to make moonshine anymore."

"Even Jesus made wine." Aulding argued.

"Well, Mister Aulding, I ain't Jesus and moonshine ain't wine." James said simply.

"You promised to deliver a certain amount of moonshine.

Some very important people know your name and there
could be trouble." Aulding threatened.

"I do not want trouble. The worst you people could do is
send me and mine to heaven. Look around you, Mister
Aulding, which place do you think would be better?" James
told him.

Aulding had no argument for that remark and so turned
his car around and forded the creek on his way back to town.
He wanted to execute vengeance on Inkle to set an example
but wisely decided to just let it drop. He could do without one
moonshiner.

Agent Smith heard about the exchange between Inkle and
Aulding and had a good laugh with Sheriff Singletree, who
had told him the whole story.

"Looks like the Lord is doing your job for you." The sheriff
told him.

"That is fine with me, I do not relish the idea of putting any
of these people in jail. I just want to cut the connection with
organized crime." Agent Smith said.

"We have to catch Aulding." The sheriff said.

"I think I can get my people to delay his driver, so maybe
Aulding will have to make a run himself. Then, we can put
him away for a while." Agent Smith reasoned.

"You take care of that and I will watch for him to leave
town. I expect he will want his special built car to make the
run." Singletree said.

Aulding's driver was picked up for 'questioning' in a
couple of days. He was extradited back to North Carolina and
essentially lost in the system for a few days. Aulding heard
the news and left to swap cars. Agent Smith had the car
stacked out and waited for Aulding to show up. Then, he
followed him north to Hatsworth. Knowing that he would be
busy making pickups, he went to contact the sheriff who was
waiting for him. They took up their positions behind a couple
of buildings beside the road leading out of town. Aulding
would have to come this way.

Aulding crisscrossed the mountain trails until he had his
load. Then, he took the one road south which lead through
Hatsworth. He saw the sheriff and another car pull from
behind the buildings and fall in behind him. He kept his speed
steady and legal until he got out of town and still did not
bring the car up to speed. At a dirt road just out of town, he
turned off and stopped at an old farm house. He pulled the
car into a barn where an identical car was waiting. Quickly,
he and his partners changed the license plates on the car.
Aulding drove the car with nothing onboard, while the other
two men drove the car loaded with illegal whiskey.

Sheriff Singletree and Agent Smith stopped on the side of
the road in a wooded area to wait for Aulding. They decided
that he must have been making another pickup. It was the
logical reason for the last minute stop.

The men who now had the load of whisky pulled back onto
the main road and headed south after Aulding. They laid
back, at a safe distance, from Aulding and the two law
officers. Aulding traveled at a leisure pass which should have
drawn suspicion from the two officers. Perhaps if they had
received some signal, some sign to tip them off they would
have been more cautious. They were speeding up to make
their stop when another car pulled along beside Agent Smith.
A man in the back seat raised up with a machine gun in his
grip. The burst of fire ripped through the door and window
of Agent Smith's car and into his body. The impact caused his
body to shake violently behind the wheel. The car veered off
the road and stopped in a cornfield, still upright.

The sheriff was intent on Aulding. He pulled along beside
him and motioned for him to pull over. Aulding obeyed. The
sheriff dropped back and pulled in behind him. He looked
around expecting to see Agent Smith pulling to a stop but
instead a car just like Aulding's pulled up beside him as he
was getting out of his car. The sheriff started to walk to the
car and tell the spectators to move along. The next thing he
saw was the barrel of a machine gun. By reflex, he reached

for his pistol but it was too late. His body would not obey. He slumped against his car and stared stupidly at the scene around him. Aulding walked to him and said something about small town sheriffs. Sheriff Singletree was thinking about his wife, Sarah. "What will she do now?" He thought as darkness engulfed him.

"Get that whiskey to the city. I will lay back and watch for cops." Aulding said coldly as they changed the license plates back.

A farmer found the sheriff slumped against his car. He loaded him on his truck and covered him with a tarp. For lack of a better place, he took him to the hotel for the doctor to look at. He had no desire to drive up to the jail where Mrs. Singletree was sure to be alone.

He pulled up at the hotel and went inside to tell the clerk to get the doctor out to his truck. The doctor came out of the hotel with his glasses in his hand. He saw the tarp pulled up with the farmer standing solemnly at the back.

"There is a car off in a cornfield down the road close to where I found the sheriff." The farmer said.

The doctor checked the sheriff for a pulse and shook his head. He went into the hotel and got a couple of men to go check on the car in the cornfield. Then, he went with the farmer up to the jail to tell Sarah. Brother Newton was there and offered to go along.

"We would be glad to have you preacher." Doctor Hill said.

Sarah was busy in the kitchen. She wiped her hands to answer the door to their private entrance. The doctor stood sadly at the door. Sarah looked over his head at the truck with the tarp on the back. She looked again at the doctor.

"Well, don't just stand out there. I was just fixing supper. I hope you can stay. We will never be able to eat all this food. I always cook to much." Sarah said with a forced laugh.

"Sarah. It is Harley. He has been shot." Doctor Hill said gently.

Sarah's eyes misted over but her conscious mind would not

accept the information.

"You are going to cause me to burn my cornbread. Please won't you all just sit down." Sarah said as she opened the stove door.

Doctor Hill stepped behind her and held her shoulders. He eased her toward a chair the preacher had pulled back from the table.

"Harley will be home any minute. Just as soon as he catches that whiskey runner. I really do not have time to sit down." She said.

"Sarah. Harley has been shot. He is dead." Doctor Hill said.

"Don't be silly Will, no one would shot Harley. Everybody likes him. Sure he would lock them up if they broke the law but they still like him." She argued.

"Sarah, let us take you down to the hotel. Bertha will take care of you." Doctor Hill told her.

"I can't leave. I have to get our supper. Harley will be home soon." She stood still then and looked the doctor in the eye.

"You've never lied to me Will. Tell me Harley is coming home." She pleaded.

"I can't tell you that Sarah. He died doing his duty. He was protecting all of us. Harley was a good man. Now, come with me to the hotel. Someone will tend your supper and close everything up for you." Doctor Hill said.

She let the doctor walk her outside.

"I'll see him now." She said as they walked near the truck.

"You don't have to, Sarah. We will take care of him." He said.

"I will see him now, Will. I must." She said.

They walked to the truck where the preacher pulled the tarp back a little for her to see his face. He looked peaceful. She rubbed his forehead as she always did.

"He is alright now." She said.

"Yes, Sarah, he is alright now." Brother Newton agreed.

Doctor Hill put Sarah in a room beside Miss Alice. He hoped that the peace Miss Alice radiated would spill over to Sarah. The men took the sheriff to the funeral home. Doctor Hill was standing on the porch when the body of Agent Smith arrived. He viewed the body and sent it to the funeral home as well.

"The feds will be all over this town now." He said to no one in particular.

Chapter

10

Trench by trench Tommy and Sparky fought the enemy
until there were no more trenches. Fresh troops were brought
up to the front to make the final drive to victory. It was time
for Tommy and Sparky to go home. Sparky and Tommy had
become good friends. A friendship forged in the heat of
battle. At times, they stood back to back, fighting for their
lives. Wounded in one battle and their forces greatly
diminished they were found sitting with their backs together
with their pistols still in their hands. Lieutenant Colonel
Hank Stanza brought his reserves up just in time to save their
lives and victory. They fought for every foot of ground.
Tommy wanted the war to end so he could go home. There
was just one way to rush things along, win the war.

The train pulled into the state capitol where Major
Bookmark and Lieutenant Patrick "Sparky" Sparks were
greeted by the Governor. It was important for the country to
have heroes after the bitter struggle. These two men were
true heroes. They did not seek hero status which made them
even more of a hero. The medals they wore were symbols of
the country's appreciation for their gallant efforts. Each man
held the memories of fallen troops under their command and

the regret of not being able to bring them home alive. They smiled at questions about the details of the war. The details of long hours in the trenches, of sneak attacks, screams of fallen men, bodies stepped over and on in the heat of battle, flashed through their mind each time. Flashes of guilt for their own survival plagued them at every question. There answer was a general one and rehearsed. They said simply that it was a hard fought war but the American spirit prevailed.

Sparky had no family back home. Tommy talked him into coming home with him and helping on the farm. They boarded the train for Hatsworth together, leaving the crowds behind. The news of their arrival somehow spread to Hatsworth ahead of them and they confronted another crowd upon their arrival home. The mayor lead the crowd in cheering for the two soldiers. Tommy stepped off the train and looked around for Marsha. He could not see her. Then the crowd opened and she walked toward him with their baby boy in her arms. She was dressed in white. The baby was wrapped in a blue blanket.

Marsha looked at her husband and a tear of joy escaped her right eye. Tommy smiled brightly as they approached. Marsha noticed something others probably did not see. The young man with the bright future and a heart filled with dreams seemed much older than he should have been after being gone just over a year. His eyes held a sadness that was not there when he left. His face had lines in it that would have been more appropriate on an older man. He looked good though. He stood proudly with his major insignias flashing in the sunlight. The two rows of medals held their own untold stories. He took her and the baby gently in his arms and held them for several minutes. He almost forgot about the crowd standing quietly around them. Tommy thought of Sparky and turned to introduce the man who had saved his life over and over. The crowd shook his hand and welcomed him to their community. Sparky breathed a sigh of relief. He had been apprehensive about making Hatsworth his new home but he felt a kinship with these people. Maybe he was home after all.

"When you get settle in, I need to talk to you." The mayor whispered in his ear.

Tommy nodded but headed for his car with his wife and child. Mister McNeil was there to open his door for him. As he was about to get in the car, he noticed James Inkle standing with his wife and daughter.

"Excuse me just a moment, Darling." He told Marsha.

Tommy walked heavily toward the family of the man who had saved his life.

"I am sorry I could not bring James home. He was a fine young man and was loyal to the end. I am proud to have been his friend." He told them.

They smiled warmly at Tommy. Mrs. Inkle stepped forward and hugged his neck. Mister Inkle reached out his big hand.

"You did the best you could, boy. You have nothing to apologize for. We are glad you are home safe." He said.

Tommy smiled at them. Finally, he felt the guilt leave his shoulders. His burdens became a little lighter. He turned toward his car with his head slightly bowed to hide the tear he brushed away with the back of his hand. Marsha took his arm and directed him to the passenger side.

"You hold the baby. I will drive us home." She said.

A loud noise like a gunshot sounded, followed by the sound of a pistol being chocked in the back seat where Sparky sat.

"It is just a backfire Lieutenant." Tommy said as he reached behind him to place a gentle hand on the weapon. Sparky relaxed and put the weapon away. Tommy wrapped his hands around the child to stop them from shaking.

Marsha missed nothing but did not mention what she saw. "Well, we better get going. I have supper on the stove. The cows have to be milked. The hogs will be starving. I will have to fed Thomas when we get home." She said cheerfully as she put the car in gear and headed up the road the few miles to the farm.

Little Thomas picked at his daddy's medals and his face all the way home, much to Tommy's delight. Sparky even enjoyed the interaction of father and son as he slowly let his body relax in the back set.

Tommy took in all the sights as they pulled into the driveway to the farm. Everything was as he had left it except for the house that stood on the hill where he had proposed to Marsha. Marsha drove past the barn and up to the new house.

"It is as you designed it." She said.

"How did you manage this?" He asked.

"It was the people of the county. Brother Newton suggested it in one of the meetings, then everybody just started making plans and donating lumber. They built the preacher a house, too, while they were at it. He was totally surprised." Marsha said.

"I am a bit surprised myself." Tommy said.

"They wanted to build it. Those who could not go to war needed to contribute to those who did go." Marsha said.

"Well, where is that supper? Thomas and I are starving." Tommy said. "What about you Sparky? Are you hungry?"

"Starving. I can smell the food all the way out here." He said.

Marsha laughed delightedly. She went around the car and took Thomas. "I will just feed the baby, then we will have supper." She said. "Tommy can show you the farm." She said to Sparky.

Marsha watched, from the house, as her husband and Sparky toured the barn and the fields near the house. Sparky was fascinated by the big fields. The cotton had been picked and sold but the corn stood ready to harvest. Thomas nestled closer as he finished satisfying his hunger. Marsha felt a deep sense of relief and joy at seeing Tommy walking around the farm again. She knew the farm was his fourth love after her, Thomas and the Lord. Of course, his writing was a close fifth.

Tommy showed Sparky the creek where they still took turns bathing in warm weather. Thomas began to smile up at her indicating that he was full. Marsha laid him down for a nap and adjusted her dress as she made her way to the kitchen to finish up supper. She was putting it on the table when the men came into the house.

"After supper, you can put your stuff upstairs. We will not be using the upstairs for a while yet." Marsha told Sparky.

The meal was reminiscent of those Tommy had eaten while staying at the McNeil's. Marsha had been taught well. The vegetables were from their own garden which Marsha had worked. The bread was from corn grown on the farm. The milk from their own milk cow. It was the kind of meal Tommy had thought about every day since he left for military duty. He hung his coat on a chair and took off his tie. Sparky hesitated to be out of uniform in the presence of his superior officer but Tommy tore down that wall immediately.

"We are no longer in the service. From now on, I am Tommy. I am just a farmer who is glad not to be dodging bullets and mortar rounds. So relax and enjoy your new home, if you will stay with us." Tommy instructed.

"I will be honored provided you let me earn my keep." Sparky said.

"On a farm, everyone earns their keep. It will be the hardest work you have ever done and the most fulfilling." Tommy said.

Sparky took off his coat and hung it on the back of his chair. The medals on both jackets held many stories that would go untold for many years to come. Marsha smiled as the two men devoured the food she had prepared. They ate as if for the first time since the war started. She was pleased. It was their first meal together in their new home.

As they were having coffee after the meal was finished, Thomas woke up and let his presence be known. Marsha went up to get him. She handed him to his daddy. Thomas looked and looked for the medals he had played with in the

car until he finally spotted them on the chair. He smiled at
the medals and then his daddy. Finally, he reached a hand
toward the colorful objects. Tommy let him touch them for a
moment.

"We will put those away until you are older. I intend to
raise a farmer, not a soldier." Tommy told his son.

"May I take him for a walk?" Sparky asked.

"I guess so. Let's ask his mother. Is he ready for a walk?"
Tommy asked turning to his wife.

"He loves the outdoors." She said.

Sparky took the excited boy out the front door into the
yard. Then, Marsha and her husband were alone together for
the first time,, since he left for the war. He reached for her
hand. She reached out her hand and rose to allow herself to
be pulled to him.

Sparky and Thomas explored the garden, the animals and
gazed at the rows and rows of corn ready to be picked.
Sparky was as fascinated as the child at all there was to see.
Here he would learn a new way of life, away from the noise of
the city and the blood of the battlefields, where he had
become a man. He had faced death many times. For some
reason, unknown to him, he had been spared to face life
afresh. It was not an opportunity he would let get by him.
Tommy, Marsha and Thomas had made him part of the
family. He would not forget their generosity. The sun lay low
in the sky turning the corn stalks to a golden color.

"Time to milk the cows and slop the hogs." Tommy called
from the front porch.

"I thought the cows put it in bottles and left it on the front
porch." Sparky joked.

"Not in the country. We have to go get it from them."
Tommy said.

Sparky carried the slop to the hogs while Tommy carried
the milk buckets with enough water to clean the cows up
before milking. Sparky noted that they smelled like he did in
the trenches and ate like he wanted to.

"Yes, but they will make some good eating this winter." Tommy assured him.

The men who had built the house had done an equally fine job on the barn. Marsha had told him about the barn. He told her in a letter to purchase two good milk cows and a couple of pigs to raise for the fall slaughter.

Milking was another experience foreign to Sparky. Tommy laughed as he remembered his first experiences with the, sometimes, aggravating animals. Sparky got swatted in the head with the cow's tail as she either swatted a fly or was just saying hello.

"Tie her tail around her ankle until you get finished. You will have to watch out for her foot, though, she will stomp it into the bucket if she can." Tommy instructed.

On the way back to the house, Tommy told him that they would have to skip their creek baths tonight because of the snakes.

"You have to always watch for snakes out here. They go for water just like other animals." Tommy said.

Sparky was a good listener. He had learned that it could be the difference between life and death. After the buckets were put away, Sparky grabbed his baggage and took it upstairs. He went to the well and drew up a bucket of water to take to his room for a bath. He was still in part of his uniform and already he had walked a baby, slopped hogs and milked a cow. He took his bath and stretched out on the soft feather mattress. He listened but heard no mortar shells. Thomas cried for a moment then was quiet. The next sound he heard was a proud rooster announcing the morning. He awoke to the smell of coffee and a mixture of cooking food. He quickly dressed and made his way down the stairs and into the kitchen. Marsha was stirring something on the stove with Thomas hanging on one hip. He appeared to be at home there and hung onto Marsha's clothes.

"Tommy is milking the cows. He said for you not to worry that you would get your turn. You can wash up on the porch while I finish up here." Marsha suggested.

Sparky went out on the back porch and poured water to wash the sleep from his eyes. Tommy came around the corner of the house whistling a hymn that Sparky had heard him whistle on the battlefields.

"I see you slept in today. The sun is almost up already." Tommy teased.

"It is the rooster's fault. He was late today." Sparky said.

"He gets up with the sun. We usually get up a little earlier." Tommy said.

They entered the kitchen to the sweet aroma of breakfast and the pleasant sound of the table being set. After a prayer of thanksgiving for the food and for being home, Tommy passed a bowl of scrambled eggs to Sparky followed by a bowl of flour gravy. Fluffy biscuits disappeared from a cloth lined basket in the middle of the table. Marsha discreetly feed little Thomas while the men ate their breakfast. She soon carried him off to his bed for another nap and joined them for breakfast.

The talk was of the farm and the happenings at the church. Marsha brought them up to date on the things that were going on in town. A deputy from the neighboring county was filling in since the death of the sheriff. The sun shined brightly through the kitchen window. Tommy saw Mister McNeil, at his house, hitching up the wagon to gather corn. It was time to go to work.

As they walked the short distance to Mister McNeil's house, Tommy instructed Sparky on the art of pulling corn.

"The corn stalks get brittle as they dry out. When you pull an ear of corn, put one hand at the base of the ear and twist it with the other hand. You can also hold it and hit it with your other hand. Sometimes you can just grab and twist but it takes practice. The mule will pull the wagon down the rows through the corn field. Sometimes we have to correct him but he pretty much knows what to do. The rows the wagon runs over are the hardest to pick because the stalks are laying over. We work as a team so do not feel bad if you fall behind." Tommy told him as they walked.

"Good morning men." Mister McNeil called to them as soon as they were in hearing distance.

"Good morning Sir." Tommy replied. "You have met Patrick Sparks. We call him Sparky."

They shook hands and Tommy led the mule toward the corn field while Mister McNeil and Sparky got acquainted. When Tommy walked too slow, the mule pushed him in the back a little to let him know there was work to be done. Tommy gave the mule a dirty look but picked up his pace to match the speed the mule seemed to want to keep. When they came to the field, Tommy pulled the reins back over the mule and draped them in easy reach. The mule set off at an easy gait. Once in a while he would help himself to a blade of corn stalk or an ear of corn. He glanced back over his shoulder to see if Mister McNeil was watching or maybe to see if they were keeping up. It was hard to tell.

The old mule got to the end of the long row of corn and made his turn, skipping two rows then walking between the third and fourth rows. Mister McNeil told the mule to woo while they picked the last of the other rows, then told him to giddy-up. By the time they reached the other end the wagon was full.

They unloaded the corn in the crib and started the process all over again. They got their third load unloaded before they looked up to see Marsha and Thomas coming to tell them that dinner was ready. Tommy grabbed the young boy in his sweaty hands and carried him to the house while Marsha hung on and tried to match his long stride.

"I have been reading about a bole weevil infestation that is making its way north." Tommy told Mister McNeil at dinner.

"What are they saying?" Mister McNeil asked around a mouth full of food. Mrs. McNeil frowned at him but kept silent.

"They are saying that the crop yield has already dropped by one-third in south Texas. It is just a matter of time before it gets to us." Tommy said. He scooped up another helping of fried squash as he talked.

"What do you think we should do?" Mister McNeil asked.

"Well, I do not want to be the one to panic. From what I have read, though, they could be here in another year. If not in the spring, then the following year." I was thinking that we should switch over to corn and cattle. The weevils do not bother corn as far as I know." Tommy said.

"I will give it some thought. There is a good market for corn." Mister McNeil said.

"I was also thinking that we could grind some of the corn, cob, shuck and all, and bag it ourselves to sell locally for feed." Tommy said.

"You have been doing a lot of thinking. Smart thinking, too, it seems." Mister McNeil said sincerely. "We have always raised cotton but I do not suppose I will miss picking it." He added.

"We better get going before Old Frank (the mule) goes to the field without us. I do believe that mule can count and tell time." Tommy said jokingly.

"He can wait a few more minutes while we have our coffee. He walks faster every year just to remind me of how old I am getting." Mister McNeil said causing laughter all around the table. "He can count, by the way. I was snaking up some logs for firewood one winter with Ol' Frank. Back then, I was an amateur with a sledge hammer and driving dogs into the logs.

Dogs are those sharp things with a flat top and chains on them. Anyway, my daddy could always drive the dogs in with no more than two swings of the hammer for each dog. It took me three or four sometimes. Well, Ol' Frank would allow me two swings per dog and then just take off to the house whether he had a log behind him or not. He would just wait there at the wood pile until I walked to get him. I hate it when a mule looks at me like he is smarter than I am." They all had a good laugh over the story. Sparky reached for the squash then noticed it was the last helping. He stopped and looked up.

"Go ahead." Mrs. McNeil told him. "Someone has to clean the bowl."

Sparky smiled and racked the fried squash into his plate. He had never had them before. It was not an item cooked in his home town.

Old Frank untied the rope he was tied with and walked over toward the porch with the rope dangling at his chin. Tommy and Sparky laughed until their full stomachs hurt. The mule stopped when he came even with the porch, pointed toward the cornfield.

Tommy and Sparky's hands were stiff from the mornings work. Blisters had formed and busted long before the dinner break. They twisted up their faces as they grabbed the first ears of corn to rip them from their stalks. It was not unusual to see drops of smeared blood on the shucks of the freshly pulled corn. They did not speak of it, losing themselves in the work and the heat of the afternoon sun. Marsha watched for them and brought fresh water to them each time they unloaded the wagon. The almost empty crib began to fill up. Mister McNeil's and Tommy's cribs would be full before the harvest was all picked. It would be time to take a load to town to sell. The grist mill owners bought corn to shell and grind for those who were not farmers. There were some cattle growers who bought corn to supplement their own supply.

Some, they would take to the mill to grind for their own needs. Nothing would go to waste.

At days end, Marsha came out with a change of clothes for herself and Tommy and a towel. They walked down to the creek to bath in the cold water. Little Thomas did not seem to notice the cool temperature of the water after his initial hard breath at touching his toes to it. The parents took turns letting him kick and play while not leaving him in the water too long at a time. Tommy soaked his cramped and blistered hands in the cold water letting the pain drift away. Still teasing and laughing, they dressed and made their way back to the house for supper. Sparky saw them coming and passed them on the way to the creek. After his first full day on the farm, he was ready to take a plunge.

Mrs. McNeil and Marsha had been canning all day. Mrs. McNeil was checking the seals on the last batch for the day when Tommy and Marsha came into the kitchen. Tommy heard the pop of lids sealing as he walked inside. They had cooked supper at the McNeil house so they could finish up the chore. Mrs. McNeil pushed a strand of slightly graying hair away from her eyes with the back of her hand.

"You children sit down. I will get supper on the table." She said.

Thomas' pawing at Marsha indicated that he was ready to eat whether anyone else was or not. He went to sleep while he was still feeding. All the playing had worn him out. Marsha put him down to take his nap then came back to help put the supper on the table. Mrs. McNeil gave her a playful stern look but appreciated the help.

Mister McNeil came in from putting up the mule just as the supper was all on the table. Their timing was impeccable after all the years of the same routine. He went to his place and waited until everyone settled into their places. Sparky was washing his hands on the porch and they waited. He rushed in and took his seat, apologizing as he did so. They thanked the Lord and ate.

With the hard work of the farm, the blisters that turned to calluses, the buildings filling with corn and hay, the predawn to after dark routine, the memories of the war were put away in the back of the two men's minds. Sparky ceased counting the ears of corn he successfully pulled without breaking the stalks. He followed the old mule pulling the wagon up and down the seemingly endless rows of corn. On the days when it rained and they could not get into the fields, he shucked corn and fed it into the sheller. Bags and bags were filled for the grist mill and to be sold. On one particular day, he was working in the hall of the corn crib alone. Mister McNeil and Tommy were out checking the property to see how many fence post they would need to fence in some of the cotton fields for pasture. A chore that would take at least all winter.

Marsha was working in the garden cutting off some late okra while Thomas sat on a blanket at the end of the row. He played happily with some of his toys. Sparky occasionally glanced at the young boy, as he fed the corn into the device to be shelled. To Tommy's dismay, Sparky still carried his revolver in a holster at the small of his back. He had not used it since coming to the farm but it still felt good there. It just felt reassuring to him to wear it, so Tommy did not push the issue.

Marsha was intent on getting the okra cut off but did glance up at Thomas to make sure he was still on his blanket. It was about dinner time. Mister McNeil and Tommy were walking up the drive toward the house. Mrs. McNeil would be putting the finishing touches on their noon meal.

The house was between the woods and the creek, so once in a while, a snake would make his way down to the creek. It was rare to see one in the yard because of all the traffic there. Sparky looked back at the child as he fed another ear of corn to be shelled. He saw something out of place. Thomas had stopped playing with his toys. He was always playing or looking down the row of okra at his mother. Now, he had turned toward the woods and was intent on something in the grass. Some instinct told the child that he was in danger. He sat upright and still. Then, over the child's shoulder Sparky saw a movement. The object grew taller and awareness came to Sparky as he left his stool and ran toward the garden. Mister McNeil and Tommy so Sparky come out of the corn crib at a dead run and knew something was seriously wrong. They, too, broke into a run toward the garden. Marsha saw the running men and started toward her child. Tommy stopped her movement.

"Don't move Marsha." He yelled as he ran.

Sparky ran to a position at the end of the garden where he had a clear view of the rattlesnake which had already curled to make his strike at the child. Sparky stopped and reached behind his back to retrieve his pistol. Tommy saw the action and put his hand on Mister McNeil's shoulder to stop him. Mister McNeil pointed at the snake in protest. Tommy pointed at Sparky as explanation.

Sparky pointed his pistol at the snake. The child had not moved but he would soon. When he moved, the snake would strike. The moment was frozen in time. A scream stuck in Marsha's throat as she stood with her mouth partially open. Sweat broke out on Tommy's forehead as he forced himself to stand very still. Then the silence was broken by a single shot. It echoed across the farm. A rooster squeaked in protest at the sudden noise. The hogs ran to the other side of the pen. Thomas turned toward his mother and started crawling off the blanket. The frozen moment was broken as all the adults except Sparky ran for the child. Sparky stood still as the smoke from his shot dissipated around him. He had seen the result of his shot as if in slow motion. The snake's head disintegrated with the impact of the lead bullet. The body of the creature flew through the air for a few feet and now wriggled in the grass, the eight rattlers sounding their, now, harmless warning.

Mrs. McNeil came to the porch wiping her hands on her apron. She heard the shot, but was, as yet, unaware of the drama that had played out in her yard. She ran to check on Thomas after seeing all the others gathered around him. She saw Sparky sitting alone.

"What is the matter?" She asked anyone who would answer.

"It was a rattlesnake." Mister McNeil said pointing to the headless creature.

"Who killed it?" She asked.

They all turned their heads toward the young man sitting alone with his head down. Mrs. McNeil walked to the young man and placed her arms around his shoulders.

"Come into the house Sparky. Some coffee will make you feel better." She said.

"I was afraid I might hit Thomas." He said.

"You did just fine. Now come with me." She said. She cuddled him as she would have one of her own as she directed him toward the back porch and the kitchen. She seated him and filled a cup with coffee for him. He sipped it, as the others entered the kitchen with the smiling Thomas. Tommy came to him and shook his hand.

"First you save my life a hundred times, now my child. I can never repay you." Tommy said.

"You already have. I have never been so happy any place." Sparky said.

"We are happy to have you here as long as you are willing to stay. We have room for another house when you are ready." Tommy said looking to Mister McNeil for approval.

"Of course, we have lots of room." Mister McNeil said as he patted his grandson on the back.

Chapter

11

The acting sheriff came to the farm to speak to Tommy about an important matter. The corn was cribbed and the garden was harvested. Tommy had settled down, with the rest of the family, to do the chores of wintertime. He had wood to cut. The fields needed to be turned under to keep them rich for future harvests. They had fence post to cut and split. As soon as the weather turned, they would need to slaughter the hogs and put the meat up or grind it into sausage. Even if they got the fence finished, it would be another season before they could stock the pasture with cattle. So, their plan was to plant it in hay and corn with the hope of selling what they did not need. Tommy invited the acting sheriff into their home where Marsha had coffee ready. After a little small talk, the sheriff got to the point.

"The governor has requested that you take over the sheriff's job by special appointment until the next election. He has authorized you two deputies of your choosing." He said.

"Sheriff, I am flattered by the governor's confidence in me but I have a whole winter of work to get done. We are converting our farm to cattle." Tommy protested.

"The governor is aware of your love for farming. He also knows you are the best man for the sheriff's job. You know the people and you have the experience you need." The acting sheriff told him.

"I have never been a sheriff. I fought Germans, but that is a far cry from being a sheriff." Tommy said.

"Mister Bookmark, we still do not know who killed Sheriff Singletree and the federal agent. We do believe that the man is still around. Organized crime is expanding all across the nation. The future of the county is at stake here. It is a question of stopping the crime activity now or having them run the county in the future. Once they get to our politicians, it will be hard to clean them out." He said.

Tommy looked at Marsha who did not show any opinion, although he knew she had one. Sparky just raised an eyebrow which did not express his opinion. They were leaving it up to him, completely.

"I have to think and pray about this. I want to talk to some people first." Tommy said.

"Exactly what we expected you to do." The sheriff said.

"I guess I am pretty predictable." Tommy mumbled.

"No, Mister Bookmark, it is not that. We are aware of your record and know that once you think something through, you take decisive action. The governor knows you pretty good." He said.

Tommy got to his feet and shook hands with the sheriff. Then, he walked him to the porch.

"I understand why you hate to leave this farm. It is a beautiful place." The sheriff said.

"A farm would not be much good, if we were afraid to go to town. I'll think about it and let you know soon." Tommy said.

"Thank you Sir." The sheriff said.

"Well, what do you think?" He asked Marsha and Sparky at the same time.

Sparky tilted his head toward Marsha indicating that she should go first. Marsha did not answer quickly. She was a smart girl and knew that they could not hide in the cocoon of their farm. They would be safe for a time but what about their children. What kind of world would they have to live in if someone did not keep crime in check? She said as much to Tommy.

"I guess we all want someone else to do the dangerous jobs. I just do not want to loss you." She said.

"My main concern is the work on the farm. I will have to be here part of the time." He said thoughtfully.

"We could both spend part of our time working here and doing the law enforcement thing. That is, if you plan to hire me as your deputy." Sparky added.

"Sure, I want you as my deputy, if I take the job. I will need to talk to Mister McNeil. I want to make sure he does not think I am neglecting my duty here. Also, I could not do it if everyone is going to sit around wringing their hands with worry." Tommy said.

They walked over to the McNeil's together. There, over coffee, Tommy explained that he understood the dangers. He also explained why he felt that the job was important. The more he talked the more he believed that he was the man for the job. He was well trained in weapons and he knew and liked people. Mister McNeil pointed out that, once the fence was built, there would be less, time-consuming, physical work to do. One man could mow hay faster than he could chop a row of cotton. He reasoned. The family listened as Tommy thought aloud of his plans for the job of sheriff. He was already thinking like he was on the job. That night, he and Marsha lay awake quietly considering the changes this could bring to their lives.

The next morning Tommy drove into town to talk to Doctor Hill. He seemed to have his finger on the pulse of the county.

"The governor wants to appoint me sheriff of the county." Tommy told him. "What do you think?"

"You are the man for the job. You are well thought of by the folks that come here. The acting sheriff is doing a good job but he is not the man to deal with organized crime." Doctor Hill said.

"Why don't we go talk to Miss Alice.?" The doctor said getting up from his chair. Tommy followed him upstairs to the old lady's room.

"Hello Miss Alice. How are you doing today?" Doctor Hill asked.

"I am doing really good. I am getting close to home." She said.

"You remember Tommy Bookmark. The governor wants him to be our sheriff. We would like your thoughts on the matter." He said.

"You want the thoughts of an old woman. Why Doctor Hill, you could do better." She said.

"You have a special insight to these things." He said.

"There is a presence in our county that was not here before." She began." It will take a strong man to drive it out. I feel that Satan has gotten a foothold. I believe it is the right time for a good man to take over the job. Mister Bookmark is a gentleman and has the insight to deal with the matter. Well, that is my opinion. I hope it helps." Miss Alice said.

Tommy reached forward to shake her feeble hand. "Thank you very much. I am happy on the farm but I want a safe place for our children to grow up. I wish only to do the right thing." He said.

"You will, Son, you will. Remember it is evil that you are dealing with. God may use you to stem the tide. Just keep the faith." Miss Alice told him.

Saturday came and Tommy walked the fields quietly praying that he would make the right decision. Marsha watched her husband as, she knew, he was agonizing over the final decision. She knew he was aware of the dangers. She knew that he was an incredibly brave man, nevertheless, still a man. Her prayers were with him as he walked and prayed. Sunday found them all in church. They had voted to name the church Clarity Baptist Church. After both, the man who donated the property and for the meaning of the word.

Brother Newton sat at the front as the congregation sang

the old hymns. Occasionally, he would rise to his feet to rejoice over some line in a song that had special meaning to him. The people had learned how to worship from him. They, too, rejoiced over the impact of their faith in their lives. As if on cue, Brother Newton took his text from Galatians chapter two and verse twenty.

"Faith
Galatians 2:20
"I am crucified with Christ: nevertheless I live; yet not I but Christ liveth in me: and the life which I now live in the flesh I live by the faith of the Son of God, who loved me, and gave himself for me."

"Faith is something that is unique to the Christian way of life. It is manifest to some degree in other areas, such as, a child having faith in its parents. But as a rule, most people live their lives based on tangible things or rather visible things. Faith to me is tangible. But to the world it is just a term that they use loosely. To a Christian, faith is the basis of our existence. Without faith, we could not go through the darkness we often pass through on our journey. Without faith, the tragedies of life would overwhelm us. It is faith that allowed us to accept the grace of God. Ephesians 3:17-19 says "That Christ may dwell in your hearts by faith, that ye, being rooted and ground in love, May be able to comprehend with all saints what is the breadth, and length, and depth and height; And to know the love of Christ, which passeth knowledge, that ye might be filled with all the fullness of God."

"We live in a world that would divert us from our faith by enticing us with the desire for physical proof, tangible proof, of our faith. We would like to see a physical hand reaching down to fix our problems. We would like to have a stack of money on the shelf for future needs. Faith, on the other hand, works differently.

"Faith is not an illusive, imaginary quality that cannot be

touched or exercised in life. It is the "substance of things hoped for."

There was more to it than that but everyone came out with a new understand of what the Bible meant by faith.

"A timely sermon, Brother Newton. It was just what I needed today." Tommy said.

"And what I needed as well." The pastor said. "I hear you may be our new sheriff."

"Yes. I have somehow found favor with the governor. I would rather farm." Tommy said.

"I suspect all those bound by duty could find something more pleasant to do. I have the blessing of doing exactly what I want to do." Brother Newton said.

"It is good to know that someday there will be no need for guns and jails and men wearing badges." Tommy said.

Marsha tugged at his sleeve and whispered. "People are waiting in line to shake the preachers hand."

Tommy looked around sheepishly at the line behind him.

"I am sorry to hold you up." He said.

A chorus of answers came back to him. All of them insisted that they were in no hurry. One man informed them politely that his chicken was getting cold. That set them all to laughing.

Aulding was not pleased with the selection of Tommy as the new sheriff. He liked it better with the acting sheriff who seemed to be honest but did not confront crime aggressively. Aulding liked the lawman that was laid back. He knew Tommy Bookmark from their meals together at the hotel. He recognized Tommy as a quiet but dangerous man, much like a coiled snake. He would spot his target and strike without hesitation. He must stop this man before he took down his operation.

He left for the city to contact his man. As he drove, he thought about the task that had been assigned to him. It was not all that hard. He had gone into the small town and sized up the people quickly. It had been no trouble to locate the moonshiners. He just followed the sugar trail. Then, the federal agent had come to town and started making waves. He was clean on that killing. No one could prove that he was connected. His trigger man had done a thorough job of eliminating the only witness. Now, he had a war hero to deal with.

Aulding found his man sitting in a bar waiting for his arrival. He was a big man, twice as wide as Aulding. His face was rough and square, like it was hewn from a tired old oak tree. The man did not smile. He sat leaning slightly forward. He made the table look small, giving the picture of a man having a tea party with his little girl. His fist encircled a bottle of beer. It, too, seemed a play thing in his big hand. Aulding had sat with the man many times but never failed to feel small and insignificant. It irritated him.

"Hello Bear." He said using the man's nickname.

"Hello Aulding." Bear said. The words gurgled up from deep inside his chest like a volcano ready to erupt.

"I have a job for you." Aulding said.

"Sure. Name it." Bear said.

"I want a small town sheriff put out of business. I do not want him killed. Just pick a fight with him and break him up real bad." Aulding said.

"Are you going to pay me or is this just for fun?" Bear asked.

"I'll pay you. You get two thousand if you win." Aulding said.

"Oh, I will win. I always do." Bear said confidently.

Aulding handed Bear a picture he had cut from the local paper. It was Bookmark in uniform.

"He is not so big." Bear said.

"No. He is tough though. Do not get in a shooting war with him. He would mow you down. Just fix him so he cannot be sheriff." Aulding said.

"Okay. If that is all you want. When?" Bear asked.

"Just wonder into town in a couple of days. Give me time to get back and settled in. Then you can set up your play with Bookmark." Aulding said.

Tommy had been working on the new fences digging post holes. He worked long hours with the diggers cutting into the earth. He dug down two feet then stepped off the proper distance and dug another hole. When the sun was high and hot in the afternoon sky, he worked in the edge of the woods splitting post from logs they had cut. He used a big ax to start the log splitting then drove in wedges with sledge hammers to finish the job. He took time to go to town and spend some time as sheriff. Sparky filled in the rest of the time. He hired another deputy to watch the jail at night.

Tommy had always been in good shape but the fencing work had put muscle on his arms and back. He stacked the fence post for transport and felt good. Marsha noticed the difference and mentioned it to him. He shrugged it off saying it was just the hard work. She doubted if he knew how strong he had become. He tossed the hardwood fence post around as if they were small sticks. He tried to work in his shirt but they kept busting at the seams. Marsha ordered him new ones from her catalog. The shoulders fit okay but the waist had to be took up some. The air was chilly so he wore a long waist coat when he went to town. His badge was pinned on the outside on the left side.

Today was a rainy day. He decided to go into town and make rounds with Sparky. He made sure Aulding knew he was in town. He had no crime to charge him with but he well knew that Aulding had something going. He lived too well and did no work that he could decipher. Aulding just smiled and gave him space.

"I am glad you are here Sheriff." Sparky said. "There seems to be a small riot down at the bar."

"I guess our vacation is over." Tommy said.

"I guess so." Sparky said.

The bar was a hangout for would-be toughs. Some of the men just stopped in to taste some store-bought brew. Others spent a lot of their time and money there. When they arrived, two men were helping each other up the street toward the hotel to see the doctor. They looked pretty bad. Tommy and Sparky walked into the bar and addressed the bartender and owner.

"What is going on here Jake?" Sparky asked.

"That city dud over there just does not like anybody. He has picked a fight with anyone who will give him the slightest excuse." Jake said.

Sparky looked at the big man sitting at a table alone. The man looked over at them as if he were waiting for them. Sparky swallowed visibly.

"You scared?" Tommy asked him teasingly.

"I ain't scared but I ain't stupid either. That is a mighty big man." Sparky said.

"Maybe, I better go talk to him." Tommy said.

"Well, you are the boss." Sparky said tilting his head to one side. "I could do it." Sparky added.

"Do you want to?" Tommy asked.

"I didn't say that I wanted to." Sparky said.

"One of us needs to talk to him." Tommy said.

"He does not look like a talker to me." Sparky replied.

"I will talk to him." Tommy said.

"Okay." Sparky replied.

Tommy gave him a stern look of reprove and walked over to the table where the big man sat. The beer in his hand seemed somehow unimportant. The man could probably drink a case and not even feel it.

"They tell me you have been causing some trouble here."

Tommy told the man.

"I had to get your attention Sheriff." Bear said.

"My attention?" Tommy asked.

"I am here on business. You are my business." Bear replied.

"I see." Tommy said looking over his shoulder at Sparky.

"Is your deputy going to bother us?" Bear asked.

"I take in my own prisoners. He will not interrupt. He may shot you if you try to get away but I will make the arrest." Tommy said.

"Well, go ahead, arrest me." Bear said.

"Stand up and turn around. Then, put your hands behind your back. You are under arrest for disturbing the peace." Tommy said.

Bear got to his feet as gently as a lamb. He started to turn as the sheriff instructed. When he was half turned, he brought up his right arm and swung it back handed at the sheriff's face. The impact sent Tommy flying across a table. He slid to a stop against the bar at Sparky's feet.

"You need any help boss?" Sparky asked.

"Yeah, hold my coat." Tommy said as he pulled off the heavy coat and handed it to his deputy. He rubbed his face. It felt like a bone was broken somewhere.

He walked back toward the big man. He had taken off his suit coat revealing that it was not fat that the coat covered. The man was incredibly strong. Bear reached down casually with one hand and grabbed a table. He sent it sailing across the room to the back wall.

"You will have to pay for that." Sheriff Bookmark told him.

"Sure I will pay. Just as soon as you get me to the jail." Bear said. While he was talking, Bear took another long swing at Tommy's head. Tommy ducked and caught the arm. Using the big man's own momentum Tommy grabbed the arm and threw the big man. His feet shook the bar as they hit it.

Bear got up with a surprised look on his face. It was the first time in his life anyone had taken him off his feet. He ran at Tommy trying to get him in a bear hug. Tommy stepped to one side pulling a chair with him as he went. Bear tripped over the chair as Tommy gave him a double-handed punch to the back of the neck. Bear fell into a clutter of chairs and tables. He came up like a wild bull knocking tables and chairs aside.

"You will have to pay for those as well." Tommy said.

"Sure, Sheriff, just as soon as you get me to jail." Bear replied.

Bear hit Tommy a vicious blow to the side of the head. Tommy turned with the punch and caught Bear with a back handed blow of his own. They stood face to face, then, exchanging blow after blow. Tommy's face took a beating but the solid right and left punches by Tommy to Bear's mid-section took its toll. Bear seemed to weaken. Sparky stood at the bar trying to look casual while he propped on one elbow. After the war, this was just good clean fun.

Tommy grabbed the big man's wrist and attempted to twist it behind his back. The arm did not move. Bear smiled broadly then made good on his bear hug. He lifted Tommy off the floor. Sparky moved from the bar but Tommy shook his head. Tommy beat down hard on the big man's shoulders. He punched sharply to Bear's face and heard the nose break. Still Bear hung on squeezing harder with each passing second. Tommy felt searing pain go up his back. He knew he could not take much more. He drew back with his arms wide and brought them together, palms open, against Bear's ears. Bear let out a scream that he, himself, could not hear. Bear bent forward and grabbed his head. Tommy dropped to the floor and rolled to a safe distance. A drop of blood ran out of one of Bear's ears.

Tommy got to his feet and walked to Sparky to get his handcuffs. Then he walked over to Bear.

"You are under arrest for brawling, destruction of private property, resisting arrest and for breaking my jawbone." Sheriff Bookmark recited through clinched teeth.

"Okay Sheriff." Bear turned around to be handcuffed. Then, he sat down on one of the chairs that had somehow stayed upright.

"I will get the doctor to look at you. I hope I did not bust your eardrum but you about broke my back. I had to do it." Tommy said.

"No hard feelings Sheriff. It was the best fight I ever had. I am sort of sorry I lost though." Bear said.

"I understand. Can you walk?" Tommy asked.

"Sparky take Bear up to the doctor's and let him look him over. If he tries to run, shot him in the knee." Tommy said loud enough for Bear to hear.

Bear gave him a hurt look like his Mama had scolded him.

"I have no intention of trying to escape. You fellows play for keeps." Bear told him.

Sparky reluctantly took Bear by the arm to direct him toward the hotel. Bear did not resist but seemed to appreciate the extra support. He had been beaten bad and he knew it. Sparky would have arrested him if told to do so. He certainly had no intention of volunteering for the job.

Aulding sat at the hotel fully expecting to see someone helping Sheriff Bookmark into the doctor's office. When he saw, the now meek, Bear being helped up the steps, he sat with his mouth gaped open. Sparky cast a stern look in his direction.

"Not who you expected?" Sparky asked him.

"I do not know what you mean." Aulding said, finally shutting his mouth.

"I bet you know what I mean alright." Sparky said.

Aulding clammed up. He could tell that the deputy was

itching for a fight. He turned away from the pair making their way up the stairs to the doctor's office. He was just getting over the challenge from the deputy when Sheriff Bookmark walked into the dining area where Aulding was having coffee. Tommy walked to Aulding without saying a word. He reached across Aulding's shoulders and picked him up bodily from his chair and shoved him out the door and around the hotel. He shoved Aulding against the chimney with his toes barely touching the ground. Aulding started to protest but that only got him slammed against the chimney harder.

"Do not talk Aulding. Just listen. I cannot prove your involvement in this matter. If I could, you would be going to jail along with your friend. I am telling you now that I will close down your operation and run you out of town, one way or the other. I was appointed to this job by the governor for one purpose and that is to keep organized crime out of this county. I intend to do so." Tommy relaxed his grip and adjusted Aulding's suit. He went inside to check on his prisoner without so much as a backward glance.

Aulding was mad. He had been called. It irritated him that he had made no effort to defend himself. Considering the minor injuries of the sheriff after his fight with Bear, a passive response seemed the safest response. He decided, then, that he would have to get rid of the sheriff some other way.

Bear was stunned but had no injuries that would not heal, except for one ear that might lose its hearing ability. Sparky took him to jail while the doctor checked out Tommy's jaw. He apparently had a crack in it but it was not broken through.

"You will be on a soup diet for a couple of months. I will give you something for the pain." Doctor Hill told him.

"Thanks doctor." Tommy said.

"I suggest you take the rest of the day off and I do not

mean to split fence post or dig holes. That kind of work could cause the bone to crack more." Doctor Hill warned.

"Yes doctor." Tommy said.

"You wiped him good. I wish I could have seen that fight." The doctor told Tommy.

"I wish you had been in it, instead of me. I hurt all over. That man is not all human." Tommy said.

"Well, you made a reputation for yourself. You will not have to fight any of the local boys for a long time." Doctor Hill predicted.

"I hope not." Tommy said through his teeth.

Tommy stopped by the jail and told Sparky the doctor's orders. Then, he drove home. Every bump in the road caused his face to hurt. He had to submit to an examination by Marsha when he got home. She made some soup for him and gave him his pain medicine.

Finally, he was in bed. He slept the rest of the day and all night through. He had expended a lot of energy and all the punches he had taken manifested themselves when he awoke for breakfast.

Chapter

12

Sheriff Bookmark found it the right thing to do to get to
know the people of the county and how they lived. Most of the
land owners were known to him by name. There was another
group of people who were a vital part of the local economy.
They lived from crop to crop, often on credit until the crops
were harvested. These people lived on a landowners property
farming it for the owner for half the profit of the harvest.
They were given a house to live in with a garden spot and
most of the time a barn and crib. It was truly a life of faith.
The sharecroppers invested their time and money in the hope
that the harvest would be bountiful. Then, they would pay off
their debts for groceries, clothes, seed, fertilizer and probably
doctor bills. There was usually not much left for Christmas
and the needs of the winter and summer until the next
harvest came in. Off-and-on, he would take some time off to
visit around the county. Time went by and Tommy settled
into his job. He did the farm work and sheriff work until the
two jobs meshed as one. Folks knew where to find him, if they
needed him.

Tommy stopped at one such family and was invited to
spend the day with them. The farmers name was Robert
Brown. His wife was named Helen. He arrived a little after
breakfast. He could smell the dried beans cooking on the
wood burning stove. The lady of the house was already

preparing for dinner. She came from the kitchen to welcome her guest with a baby on one hip and a two year old hanging onto her skirt. Her hair was pulled back from her face She smiled a weak but pretty smile. Her hair was already turning gray although she could not be over thirty years old.

Betty, a teenaged girl sat on an upside-down bucket shucking corn to go with the dried beans. Her name was Betty. She wore a long homemade skirt with a boys shirt for a blouse. Her shoes had thick soles and many laces. They were purchased to protect her feet not for their beauty. She was a pretty thing. Tommy had not seen her at church. Perhaps, she attended one close by. There was not a family car or truck. These people were trapped in the world of their farm, which was not even theirs. A younger girl, named Lilly, stood with her sister watching the corn shucking process. Sometimes she would pull at the shucks on an ear of corn to help her sister but the task was too difficult for her tender hands. She picked up a bunch of corn husk. It was golden except for the ends which had turned a dark brown. While her older sister worked intently, Lily tickled her sister under the nose with the husk. The teenage girl scolded her sister and wiped the tickle from her nose with the back of her hand. The knife she was using passed dangerously close to her face but her hands were practiced and she was in no danger.

Two boys came down the little farm road from the barn leading two milk cows. They each carried a bucket of milk in one hand while they lead their cow with the other. The cows had long pointed horns which the boys used to shove the cow's head around if they got too close to their back side. They stopped in front of the house. The older of the two boys, William, took the ropes of both cows while the younger boy, Jesse, carried the two buckets of milk into the house by the kitchen door. He, of course, teased his sister has he passed back by, empty-handed. He flipped her hair over her head into her face and dodged to avoid the hand with the knife in it. She would not have cut him on purpose but her reactions were quick. By the time everyone got through teasing her and she was finished with shucking the corn, she had corn on her face and in her hair. The younger of the two girls picked up the basket full of shucks and carried them down to the pasture to give the cows an extra treat.

The boys came back to the house but did not sit down to rest. The younger of the two grabbed up the slop bucket and headed around the smokehouse to feed the hogs. The elder son took up an empty bucket and headed off past the garden to the well. He had to draw up the days drinking water and fill a barrel for washing clothes. Jesse finished slopping the hogs first, so he had a little time to help his sister get the corn into the house.

Tommy was following along behind the husband and daddy of the family. He was following an old mule through a potato patch. The plow he sunk deep into the earth turned up the rows of potatoes leaving the potatoes laying on top of the ground. A stack of baskets sat at the corner of the field waiting for young hands to take them up. The boys made their way to the field together and grabbed up a basket each. Without being told what to do, they bent to the task of picking up the potatoes and swishing around the dirt to look for any they missed. They carried full baskets to the end of the field and picked up an empty one to be filled. Tommy saw what they were doing and grabbed up a basket to help out. They did not object, neither did Tommy mind doing the work. It was the way of the farm. If work needed to be done, a man, or a boy, just naturally put his hands to doing it.

The morning passed without being noticed. The sun rose high in the sky. Robert came to the end of a row and drove the mule to a shade near the barn. He went into the barn and came back with a chunk of hay for the mule then went to the well with a bucket from the barn and brought back a bucket of water. The boys did not stop picking up potatoes until their daddy came back through the field and told them it was time to eat. As Robert walked over the ground they had picked, he used his toe to flip potatoes from under the earth.

"We will bust these rows again, just to make sure we get all of them." He said as his long legs stretched over the humps of dirt.

Tommy stepped on top of the humps only to have them collapse under his weight. He learned why the farmer stepped over them.

The boys grabbed up a basket each of potatoes and carried them to the house on their way. Tommy and the farmer did the same. Tommy sat the basket where the boys had put theirs then straightened up too quickly. He felt a piercing pain shoot through his lower back. He groaned aloud. The boys were both pushing their fist into the small of their back and standing slowly to their full height.

"Stand up slow." The older boy said. "That way, it don't hurt as much."

The farmer washed his hands in a pan of water placed on the back porch for that purpose. There was a water bucket on a small shelf with a wash pan along side. He flipped the water into the yard and poured some fresh for his guest.

"There you go Sheriff, wash up and we will have some dinner." He said.

Tommy washed the dirt off his hands trying to get the stubborn bits from under his fingernails. The boys waited for him with subdued impatience. The water Tommy was using turned the color of earth so he decided he had done all he could do. He reached for the towel hanging on a nail but the teenage girl handed him a fresh one. She smiled beautifully at him and he returned the smile with a thank you. She giggled slightly and straightened her skirt. She pushed her hair back behind one ear. Then her mother called for her and she was gone. The little one had followed her sister to the porch and still stood staring up at Tommy. Tommy reached for her hair and gave one curl a little tug. She immediately ran back into the house.

"Mommy, the sheriff pulled my hair." Lilly tattled.

"Well, he wasn't trying to hurt you." Her mother told her.

"It didn't hurt none. Sister was flirting though." She said.

"I was not. I just took the sheriff a towel like Mama said." She defended.

"You two hush and get the food on the table. Anybody would think you had never seen a man besides your daddy." She said to the girls as she smiled up at Tommy.

"All of you be quiet now. Your Mama is going to pray." The farmer said to his children.

Mama did pray. She prayed that the food would be blessed. She prayed for the crops and that the children would not get sick. The farmer patted her on the shoulder when she was finished.

"Okay, Sheriff, such as it is, dig in." Robert said.

"It looks delicious." Tommy said.

"We growed everything." William said.

"We grew everything." Mama corrected.

"Yes we did." The older boy said.

"She means you ain't suppose to say 'growed'." Betty said.

"Well, you ain't suppose to say ain't neither but you did." William replied.

"Be quiet and eat." The farmer said. "At least, don't argue."

The meal was a country feast and already the boys ate like grown men. After all, they were already doing a man's work. Tommy enjoyed the meal and the company of these humble people. They were God-fearing and honest in their ways. He also prayed that their crops would do good.

The farmer gave the children a half hour of free time to let their dinner settle down. We sat on the porch with a cup of coffee. His wife rocked and nursed the baby just inside the door. The younger of the two boys brought out his arrowhead collection for Tommy to look at. He had a wide variety. Some of the white flint was especially well shaped.

"We find them all the time but the best time is in a plowed field after it rains. The rain pushes down the dirt around the arrowheads. I also have some pottery you can look at some time." Jesse told him.

Too soon, it was time to start picking up potatoes again. Tommy helped the boys carry those already picked back to the house while the farmer went for his mule. The farmer's wife left the younger girl to watch the baby while she and Betty went to do the washing. The fire had been started in the morning under the wash pot, so the water was boiling hot now. They dipped the clothes into the hot water and swished them around with a stick that looked suspiciously like an ax handle. Then, they would dip them in cold water to cool them and give them their first rinsing. With the clothes cooled, they could give them a finally rinsing in another tub and squeeze out the excess water. Some of the delicate clothes were washed by hand in a tub using a rubboard to gently remove the soiled spots. Tommy glanced up at the women going about the task and was glad he was picking up potatoes. The clothes were carried to clothes lines near the house to be hung up to dry in the afternoon sun. Dishes rattled in the house as Lily cleaned up the kitchen while checking on the little one every few minutes.

Tommy bent to his work. There was little conversation but he was learning a lot the hard way. He was here for a visit but these people did this work day after day and year after year. Still, they remained poor. The land owner had several families working his farm, each providing him some profit each year. His work included the bookkeeping and logistics of ordering seed and fertilizer. The land owner also raised cattle to sell at the market. The sharecroppers helped him look after them as part of their daily routine but received no profit from those efforts. Their reward was a place to pasture their milk cows and the old mule.

Of course, there was the free rent, if free was the right word. The house was a shelter and nothing more. The wind blew through the rafters in the winter and the flies found their way in during the summer. Sometimes the farmers wife would get all the children in the house with towels and shirts and start in the back rooms to chase the flies outside. The front door would be opened in advance and they beat the air and around the windows until the flies fled toward the doors in terror. Then the doors were quickly shut leaving them relatively fly free for a spell.

Finally, they had all the potatoes picked up from the ground that had been turned. The sun was going behind the trees as they carried the last baskets to the house. The boys left, immediately, to retrieve the cows for the evening milking. Then there was the slopping of the hogs and water to be drawn for the night baths, such as they were. The boys hated nights like tonight. The girls were taking full baths, so they had to carry water to the house to fill up a tub for them. A kettle of water was on the stove to take the chill off of the well water. Supper was finished before they finished, so the family sat down to eat. Mama talked to God and they all ate. Tommy lifted his fork tiredly to his mouth. It had been a very long day.

"I am going to let the boys have the day off tomorrow if you would like to spend the night. They can show you their swimming hole and maybe we can get in a little fishing. Mama and the girls may even walk down and join us." Robert said.

"I am too tired to drive tonight so I guess I will stay if it is not too much trouble." Tommy replied.

"It will be no trouble. You can sleep in the living room. We have some quilts to make you a pallet to sleep on. You will have to sleep in your clothes though with the girls in the house." Helen said.

"That will be fine. I have some extra clothes in the car, so I can change." Tommy said.

After supper was finished, Tommy went out to the well and drew up some water to wash off the days sweat and dirt. He was in amazingly good physical condition but the boys had worked just as hard as he had worked. He wondered how their slim bodies did the work they had to do. The well water was cold but in the night air it felt slightly warm to him. He could hear the farmer's wife singing some old hymn as she worked in the kitchen. The girls were apparently already sharing a tub of water. The boys were on the back porch washing their feet before they went to bed. The farmer came to the well and pulled off his shirt. He had no fat on his bones. He scrubbed the dirt and sweat off his muscled-chest, then picked up the tub with the remainder of the water and poured it over himself. He would wash his feet on the back porch as the boys were doing. Sometime after the family was all settle in, the farmers wife made her way to the well to wash herself. She carried an old bed sheet to give her some privacy just in case. But it was dark by now and only the lightening bugs kept her company. Tommy lay on his pallet and heard her return to the house just before he dropped off to sleep.

Saturday was usually just another hard workday for the sharecropper family. Since the sheriff was there, the farmer decided to give the boys the day off. There was always something to do, but it was not quiet time to pick the cotton. Sometimes, between the time they stopped fighting Johnson grass and weeds, and harvest time there was a few days they could take off. Today was such a day. The boys got up early, as usual, to milk the cows and slop the hogs. Tommy jumped from his pallet and wished that he had not. His whole body hurt all at one time. He sat down in a chair to let the pain subside. The farmer's wife giggled a little at him. She was sitting in the rocker feeding the baby. Tommy had not heard her come into the living room.

"I never knew I could be so sore." He said.

"We grow up doing this kind of work. Our body knows nothing else." She said with understanding.

"Breakfast is ready." She said adjusting the baby. "We will eat when the boys get back from milking."

"Maybe I will just walk around outside for a bit." Tommy said.

"Might be good to put your shirt on. The girls will be up in a minute. The oldest already thinks you are something but she knows you are married. I do not want her hormones going crazy just yet." The lady said without any foul meaning.

Tommy had forgotten to put his shirt on because of the pain that shot through him when he jumped up too fast.

"Yes ma'am. Sorry." He said.

He looked at her, then turned away blushing. She was switching sides with the baby.

"Don't be embarrassed Mister Bookmark. I have been feeding babies for fifteen years. It is God's way and nothing to be ashamed about." She said.

"Of course not ma'am. I will just go stretch my legs." Tommy said.

"Just come in when the boys do. We will eat then." She said.

Tommy went outside to the sound of the farmer's wife singing softly to the baby. The farmer came into the living room buttoning his shirt.

"The sheriff is a little shy, isn't he?" Robert said after overhearing the conversation.

"He is a gentleman. I am glad there are still men who blush once in a while." She said.

"He seems to be a good man." The farmer said.

The boys turned the cows into the pasture and Tommy followed them into the kitchen. He shied away from the living room just in case the baby was still eating. The baby had been put down and the family all gathered around the table for the morning meal. The farmers wife prayed and the biscuits disappeared from the bowl into plates around the table. She had prepared two bowls of flour gravy which now made their way around the table in hungry hands. There was sausage and eggs to round out the feast. The farmer liked red-eye gravy on top of his flour gravy. Tommy tried it and was spoiled for life. He asked the lady how it was made and filed the receipt away so he could tell Marsha.

"You boys can take the sheriff fishing this morning. We will eat dinner and then go swimming after our dinner settles. You boys wear your shirts at the swimming hole. The girls will be coming down today." The farmer said.

The oldest of the girls looked at Tommy probably imagining something about him without his shirt.

"You are staring, young lady." The farmer's wife scolded her.

The girl turned her eyes back to her food then sneaked one more look.

"Sister is staring again." The younger girl tattled.

"Be quiet and eat your breakfast." Mama said.

Tommy and the boys went across the hill behind the house. They walked through a pine thicket then down a steep hill. The ground leveled and they were among some great old trees at the river's edge. Squirrels played in the trees and barked at them as they readied their fishing poles. Each of the boys had two poles. They drove one cane back into the bank and held the other one. Tommy watched the boys then sat down to watch his own line. The boys wore no shoes. They dug their feet into the sandy shore of the river. The water ran slow and quiet here. It had a green tint except where the trees shaded it. There it looked black and mysterious. It was hard to imagine how deep the water might be. Tommy was sure it would be at least twelve feet deep. Tree roots sprouted out of the banks into the water. It would be a dangerous place to fall into the water. Tommy dug his feet into the sand. He felt more secure. His cane bent toward the river. He had a strike. He held still until the cane bent again. He jerked the pole slightly to one side and hooked the fish. The boys called it a blue-cat. It was a meal in itself. They all laughed as Tommy 'wrestled' with the big fish trying to put it on a stringer. He let the fish drop back into the water and secured the stringer around a root. While he was baiting his hook a second time, one of the boys pulled in a fish of his own. They were having a good morning.

"Looks like we will be having fish for dinner today." William announced.

"Yeah. It has been two weeks since we had fish." The other said.

"What about squirrel?" Tommy asked.

"We kill a few, now and then, but there is not much meat on them. I would rather watch them play." The older boy said.

"I like rabbit better." Jesse said, then they all got quiet and returned to their fishing.

Back at the house, they cleaned their fish and Robert set them to cooking in plenty of time to have them ready for dinner. He had a small pot in the kitchen yard into which he poured canola oil. He dropped the fish in the hot oil and in no time at all they were ready for the table. Helen was getting the fixings ready to go with the fish.

The swimming hole was another story entirely. The locals called it 'the island' because of the small spot of untended land which was surrounded by a slough and the river. It was a snake invested area and no one ventured anywhere except on its very edges. The story was that it was planted in corn in years gone by. The swimming hole was formed where a large tree leaned out in the river and let its limbs drag in the water. The water rushing under the limbs dug out a nice deep hole.

Just below the swimming hole was a wide shallow expanse.
The water was very swift for a quarter of a mile. You could
walk right up to the edge of the swift water and stand in knee
deep water. The moment you stepped into the swift water,
you were fighting to stand. It gained speed as it fell down the
rocky bottom incline and disappeared around a curve in the
river. Some had ventured down the incline. One man was
caught in the water and had his cutoff overalls torn from his
body.

There was a narrow trail from the nearby cotton field
through the trees to the river. A sink hole had developed
about halfway down the trail and had to be skirted. The trail
was a road at one time long ago. Down at water level part of a
pole bridge could be seen, now covered by tons of river sand.
Just the ends stuck out. The trail led down to the water's edge
where the slough branched off to go around the island. The
water in the slough looked rusty and skimmed over, after it
sat for a while without the river feeding it. When the river
was at flood stage, it ran around the slough with roaring
speed and often spread out into the surrounding fields. It was
a frightening sound to hear the river as you walked down the
trail through the trees. In those times, it would run red with
the clay dirt from upstream.

Today it was moving lazily except for the swift water and
was clear as could be with a green tint. The boys climbed into
the tree and after yelling loudly jumped into the cool water.
Robert and Helen walked down the trail and waded out a
couple of feet to let the babies get their feet wet. Betty and
Lilly ventured out to their waist. Well, it was to Betty's waist.
Lilly hung on to her sister and tilted her head back to breath.

"Bring your sister back this way some." Robert told Betty.
Lilly breathed deeply when she had the water off her chest.
"Are you trying to drown me, Sister?" Lilly scolded Betty.
"You have to learn to swim sometime." Betty replied.
"You go out there and swim back to us, Betty, and show
your sister how it is done." Helen told her.

Betty backed out into the water until it came up to her chin. She kicked at the bottom and came to the surface in full stride, making her way to shore in a cloud of splashing water. Betty was well covered, as was their custom, but the water nullified her efforts. Tommy decided, then and there, that if he had a daughter, she would not swim with boys who were not her brothers.

"Get back in the water Betty, we have company." Robert told her.

One of the boys was going to the bottom and bringing up all shapes and shades of beautiful rocks. It seemed he stayed under forever. Robert seemed to watch all his children at once. He enjoyed watching them have fun. They had little enough fun, working like they did. Lilly backed out into the river and splashed back to shallow water like her sister had done. She swam smooth and unafraid. Someday she would be a good swimmer. William climbed to a high limb and announced his intention to dive.

"Do not go to deep." Robert cautioned.

"Yes sir." William replied and sailed into a perfect dive and cut the river water with only a little splash. He came up with a speckled rock which he tossed to Jesse.

Betty came over to get the two year old and took her out a few feet to play. She was very careful and did not tease her like she did Lilly. Betty held her flat on the water's surface and let her splash. Lilly was copying her brother and going under for rocks. Somehow the five children survived the day of fun. Robert cautioned them here and there but, mostly, just let them play. He had Betty come to shore to watch the two babies and then took Helen out for a short swim. For a few minutes, she was a child again. She frolicked in the water and splashed water at her husband. Helen was a good swimmer and even climbed up on the tree to show off her diving skills. She was a beautiful woman. Burdened with a lot of responsibility but beautiful under all the strain.

The time of fun ended as Robert and Helen came out of the water and shouldered their responsibilities again. Helen gave Robert one last splash and he chased her all the way to shore trying to splash her in retaliation. She was too fast for him. Tommy grabbed up the two year old and headed up the trail. Robert took the baby, to let Helen rest for a while on the way back. Tommy had gotten water in his ears and was trying to let it drain out by tilting his head to one side. William picked up a warm rock from the edge of the cotton field and handed it to Tommy.

"Hold it on your ear for a little bit. It will evaporate the water out." He said.

He was right. That was a trick well worth remembering.

Tommy suddenly got very homesick. He had been gone only a couple of days but it was the same feeling he had when he was overseas in the military.

"I have to leave." He told them on the way back.

"You are welcome to stay and go to church with us tomorrow. We go to the little white church up the road." Robert said.

"How do you get there?" Tommy asked.

"We walk. It is only two or three miles." Robert replied.

"I will go home. I am afraid, I miss my family. I have a son who needs to learn to swim. He may not be old enough to swim but I can get him use to the water." Tommy said.

"That is the best way. Start them while they are young and they will not be afraid." Helen added.

"When are you coming back, Tommy?" Betty asked.

"Mister Bookmark." Helen corrected.

"When are you coming back, Mister Bookmark?" She asked correctly.

"I am not sure. I want to visit a lot of people in the county.

Maybe I will bring my wife next time." He told her.

"Oh, you don't have to bring her." Betty said sadly.

"Betty Brown! You run on ahead and go to your room. I will speak to you when I get there." Helen said.

Tommy looked out across the field to divert his eyes from the teenage woman. She was a sight to behold. She dared to look over her shoulder one last time to see if Tommy was looking. He was not. All Betty saw were her parents, both with faces of granite.

"She is a mess." Robert said after she was out of hearing distance.

"Girls grow up fast on the farm. She has been tending youngsters since she could walk and doing a woman's work, almost as long. I expect she is about ready to marry, although we will sorely miss her." Helen said.

"If that be the case, I have a young deputy who is single and would be a good provider. He also likes farming. Maybe I could bring him over sometime." Tommy ventured.

"That would be fine if he does not mind sitting with her while her parents look on." Robert said.

"He won't mind. He is a fine man." Tommy said.

Tommy gathered up his belongings and put them in the car. Betty peeped out the window at him as he loaded the car. Robert came out with a basket of potatoes for him. It had been a good visit and Tommy felt as if he was leaving family.

Not too many miles up the road, his own family was waiting. It would be good to be back home. He swung through town to check on Sparky and the deputy. It was time for shift change and so Sparky rode home with him. Tommy told him about the pretty girl he had found down in the south end of the county.

"She is like a wild flower, not yet discovered, but beautiful just the same." Tommy told him.

Marsha saw them coming and scooped up the baby and ran across the yard to where Tommy parked the car. She did not wait to be grabbed but threw her arms around Tommy as he was getting out of the car. Thomas was squeezed in the middle. He laughed at the sudden activity and pawed at his daddy.

Sparky grabbed two milk buckets and headed to the barn. He hollered at Tommy over his shoulder.

"I got the chores tonight. You just enjoy being home." He said.

"Thanks Sparky." He said as he put his arm around Marsha's waist and walked to their home. The smell of supper greeted him.

Chapter

13

Doctor Hill was at the McNeil place before breakfast. He drove up to Tommy and Marsha's house and knocked on the door. Marsha answered the door with the baby in her arms. She had been feeding him.

"I need to see Tommy right away." The doctor told her.

Marsha did not hesitate. She had never seen the doctor so worried. She ran with the baby into the bedroom where Tommy was getting dressed.

"The doctor is here." She said. "He looks worried."

"Get us some coffee." Tommy said.

The doctor sat nervously in the living room on the edge of a chair. He arose when Marsha came into the room.

"I have coffee in the kitchen. Please come with me. Tommy will be here shortly." She said.

The doctor followed her into the kitchen. She placed a cup of coffee in front of him. She swung Thomas on the hip away from the hot coffee. Sparky came in with the morning's milk and sat it on the counter.

"Good morning Doctor. What brings you out this way?" Sparky asked.

"We have had trouble in town. I will tell you and Tommy at the same time." He said.

Tommy came in buttoning his shirt. He poured his own coffee and went to sit down across from the doctor.

"Your deputy has been shot." The doctor said abruptly.

"How is he?" Tommy asked fearing the worst.

"He is dead, Tommy. He was riddled with bullets. It does not look like one of our people did it. They mostly use shotguns." Doctor Hill said.

"Where is he now?" Tommy asked.

"We took him over to the funeral home. His mother has been told. As you know, he was not married. His father died a couple of years back." The doctor said telling Tommy things he already knew very well.

"I will go into town. Sparky you stay here and look after my family. Someone may be on a shooting spree. Keep the shotgun handy. Even if you have to let some work go, stay near the house. Get one of my pistols and put it where Marsha can get to it." Tommy ordered as if they were back in the army.

"They're my family too, Tommy." Sparky said.

"Yes. Of course, they are. I may be gone for a while. Go ahead and go to church." Tommy said.

"Please be careful." Marsha said.

"I will." Tommy said as he left for town without breakfast.

"He is mad, isn't he Sparky?" Marsha asked.

"Yes ma'am. As mad as I ever saw him. Do not worry, he will be methodical and careful but I would not want to be the person who shot the deputy." Sparky said. "I will get those guns now."

"Thank you, Sparky." Marsha said in a hushed voice.

Tommy went to the funeral home to view the body of his deputy. He pulled back the sheet to see the body of a man riddled with bullets. The wounds went across his body in a horizontal line, the bullets piercing his heart and lungs. He did not have a chance. Tommy visualized the deputy sitting at the desk in the jail and turning to see who had entered the office. Then a man standing there with a machine gun waiting for the look of terror that must have crossed the deputies face. Perhaps the deputy reached for his pistol which would have been blocked by the arms of the chair. Regardless, he would not have had time to return fire. It was a hit intended to shock the sheriff's department. It was a message from organized crime to tell the sheriff that it was hands-off the activities of organized crime in the county.

Sheriff Tommy Bookmark went to the mayor's home. Without preamble, he told the mayor that he wanted an ordinance against machine guns in the city and county.

"I want legal right to arrest anyone carrying such a weapon in the town and county. These men will be back and I want to arrest them before they start shooting." Tommy said.

"I can help you with the town but I have no authority in the county." The mayor said.

"Do me a favor and get hold of the commissioner. Explain what has happened. I am sure you two can work out a joint ordinance." Tommy said.

"I am sure we can Sheriff. I am sorry about the deputy." The mayor said.

"Me too. Tell Sparky when the ordinance is in force. I have to go to the city for some business." Tommy said.

Tommy left the office the way he came in. The mayor breathed a sigh of relief as the door slammed.

"I am glad he is not mad at me." He said aloud to himself. "The sheriff has declared war."

Monday morning, Tommy drove to the city to see the governor. The secretary insisted that he needed an appointment. Tommy told her to tell the mayor that Sheriff Tommy Bookmark was there to see him. She entered the mayor's office to pass along the message. Tommy followed close on her heels. She turned to block his way.

"I am sorry sir. You cannot just barge into the governor's office." She said.

Tommy walked past her to a few feet in front of the governor's desk. The governor was on the phone but he informed the party that he would call them back.

"I will have to call security." The secretary said.

"Call whoever you like, ma'am, I am not leaving until I finish my business." Tommy told her. He carried his revolver on his belt and it did not go unnoticed by the secretary.

"That is alright Linda. Mister Bookmark has a standing invitation to see me at any time." The governor told her.

"Will you be alright sir." She said, indicating the firearm.

"I will be fine." He said.

"Thank you for seeing me." Tommy told him.

"I seem to have no choice. I can see why the Germans retreated." The governor said with a small laugh.

"Sorry about my rude entry. I do not have time to waste with niceties." Tommy informed him.

"So, tell me what is on your mind." Governor Sam Perks said.

"I have just had a deputy shot down while sitting at his desk in the jail. It was a an obvious hit by someone who wanted me to get a message. A message to stay out of their business." Tommy said.

The governor sat back in his chair. A security officer opened the door and looked in. The governor waved him out.

"I told you when you took the job that I would give you what you needed to do it. So what do you need?" Governor Perks asked.

"I need to be deputized as a federal revenue agent. I intend to pursue the killer and those who sent him to my county. The men will be brought to justice or justice will be rendered where I find them if they so choose." Tommy told him.

"I do not have that authority." The governor said.

"You have friends or you would not be in your position. Cut through the red tape and get me the appointment. I need it today." Tommy said.

"You do not waste around." Governor Perks said.

"I do not have time. I am going back home to see the

widowed mother of my deputy. I intend to make her a promise. I do not make promises lightly Governor. I want the authority to carry out my promise." Tommy told him.

"Then, to keep my promise to you, I will make some calls." Governor Perks said.

"I will wait." Tommy said and slide back in his chair to do just that.

"I meant, I would do some calling during the day." The governor explained.

"It is during the day, now, Governor." Tommy replied.

The governor pushed his intercom and told Linda to bring in a pot of coffee and to get a particular senator on the phone. Tommy sat patiently drinking his coffee while the governor did his thing. He was indeed a master of politics. Apparently, a lot of people owed him favors. The governor worked the men he talked to like a chess master works the board. Tommy was making plans as he sat quietly waiting. The coffee was pretty good and so it was not long until he had to find a restroom. The governor liked the man but was relieved to have his office back, if only for a couple of minutes. The sheriff was a bomb that was going to go off in someone's face. The governor did not want it to be his face. Governor Perks was glad to hear Linda's voice saying that the senator was on the line. Tommy walked past her desk as she passed the message to the governor. He smiled sweetly to her. She frowned with her eyes but gave the necessary smile with her lips. Her turf had been invaded and she did not like it. She was the gatekeeper to the governor's office and Tommy had breeched her authority. Tommy entered the governor's office to be greeted by a smile on the governor's face.

"You can pick up your badge and papers at the local office of the federal revenue service. They are working on them as we speak." Governor Perks said.

"I will need the address." Tommy said.

"Not necessary. They are across the street. Let's give them

a few minutes while we finish off this coffee and talk about your county. You would frighten those people sitting over there. They are just pencil pushers, not a warrior like yourself." Governor Perks said.

"I understand. The coffee is good. I do not mean to come off like a warrior. I believe in law and order AND peace for the sake of our children and grandchildren. I do not like bullies. Germany tried to be a bully. Organized Crime is a bully. I do not like bullies." Tommy said.

"The coffee is good today." The governor said, hoping to calm the storm that was brewing.

Tommy went through the formality of being sworn as a special agent for the federal government. The young officer who performed the brief ceremony had received a call from the secretary and was scared out of his wits by the county sheriff's presents. Tommy tried to make it easy for him but the young man's hand still shook when he handed Tommy his badge. Tommy did not see himself as an imposing person. He was gentle until pushed to his limit. Yet standing there in his uniform with the well-used pistol ready at hand, he was imposing. As he moved to sign the documents, his muscles flexed against the uniform shirt. When he shook the sweating hand of the young officer, his hand was hard and calloused. The young officer decided that this man would exact justice with or without the badge and wondered at what might have happened had he not gotten what he wanted. Little did the young man know that he was witnessing a legend in the making.

Tommy wasted no more time. He drove back to Hatsworth planning his strategy as he drove. His deputy was ready for viewing when he got into town. He went to the funeral home to talk with the deputy's mother. It was not an easy task.

"I am very sorry about your loss. I promise you that I will find the killer and those responsible for your son's death. If you need anything, let me know personally. You will be taken care of. Your son was a good man." Sheriff Bookmark told the widow.

"Thank you Sheriff. I know you will do your best." She said.

People began to file in to see the young man in his coffin. His mother dutifully shook the hands of those who offered sympathy. She would break down later in the privacy of her home. Now, she must be strong for a few more hours.

The young man was buried at Clarity Baptist Church. It looked like the entire county turned out for the funeral. The windows were raised so those standing outside could hear the service. As the dirt was shoveled over the casket, Tommy went to sit in his car waiting for Marsha and Thomas. Sparky accompanied them back to the car. His eyes were ever searching for strangers. Sparky was not nervous. He was just ready. There was no thought of giving his life for the sheriff's family. His only thought was that they would be protected, no matter what.

The drive home was a silent trip except for Thomas who was seldom ever still anymore. He had a tooth trying to come through, so he was between overactive and crying over his sore gums. Tommy got his wife and child into the house and announced that he would be back in a while. He walked back into the forest behind their house. He climbed the mountain, sometimes holding onto trees to pull himself higher. High above the farm he found a perch on an outcropping of rock. He sat down on the rock and looked out toward the west and the setting sun. Then, he looked up to heaven while tears ran down his face. He did not reach to wipe them away. He wept for the fallen deputy and the job that was ahead of him. He wept because all he really wanted to do was farm and write his book. Would he always be defending the freedoms he cherished so much? Would he ever be able to rest?

He found no particular answers. He remembered the young man as he lived, so anxious to please. He remembered the mother who was trying to be so brave. He remembered the words from some book he had read, someplace, sometime that "freedom was not free." The question came as a groan from his soul, "How long, Oh Lord?" Did he hear an answer or was it just the very real thought of a writer? "Until the battle is done." The words rang in his head.

"I have never seen Tommy like this." Marsha told Sparky in the kitchen.

"I saw him like this once before. It was when young James Inkle died saving his life. He often wondered aloud why he was spared and such a fine young man was dead. Dead to save him. I guess he feels the same about the deputy. The killing was just a message meant for your husband. Tommy knows that. He is blaming himself. He will find his answer then he will finish the job." Sparky said making one of his longest speeches since living with them.

"I hope it does not destroy him." Marsha said.

"Not him. He has too much to live for but someone will pay the price for murder. He will be the old Tommy, but not until he finishes the job." Sparky added.

Tommy came down from the mountain. He could barely make out the path but he knew it well and handed himself from tree to tree where necessary. He found his wife and friend sitting in the kitchen.

"I think I will have something to eat." He said.

Marsha jumped up at once. She was immediately upset with herself for not thinking of food already.

"I will fix something." She said.

"I will help you while Sparky volunteers to do the milking." Tommy laughed the laugh of peace with the course he had set for himself.

"I quit volunteering when the war was over but I will get to eat sooner if you both work on supper." He said going out the door.

"What will happen?" Marsha asked.

"I will uphold the law, nothing more. There are murderers out there. They may hide behind machine guns or in suits behind some business. I will find them and then I will be home." He said.

"When will you leave?" She asked.

"Tomorrow." He said.

"I am afraid." She said.

"Don't be. Our faith is most important when we need it most. Just keep the faith." He told her.

Marsha turned to him and buried her face in his shoulder. He held her for a long time then they turned back to the stove. Supper was almost done.

Tommy packed his pistols except for the one Marsha might need. He packed a pump shotgun with a box of ammunition. He threw in a couple of suits and took the load to his car. He talked to Sparky at length in the yard before he went to the house to say goodbye to his wife. He told Sparky again to let work go, if necessary to protect his family. He told him about the Brown family and to see about getting them to work some during the winter while Sparky was doing the sheriff duties. During those times Mister McNeil would keep watch. With only one road to the house, it would be hard for anyone to surprise them. The steep mountain behind the house provided a natural barrier on that side. With all the instructions given, he went back to the house to say goodbye. Marsha was feeding Thomas. She had done her crying in secret. Now, she smiled sweetly at her husband. It was a picture Tommy would cherish in the times ahead of him.

Sheriff Bookmark found Aulding in his hotel room. He was dressed like a business man. His suit was immaculate. Tommy wore his jeans, a brown shirt and his big coat with the badge on it. Aulding started to greet the sheriff but then realized that he had not knocked before barging into his room. It galled him.

"You can't just walk into a man's room." Aulding said.

Tommy hit him so hard that it sent Aulding out the window and onto the porch over the well area. Aulding tumbled off the roof into the puddle where people threw their wash water. He got up slowly trying to wipe mud off his new suit. He rubbed his jaw with a mud-caked hand. He went to the porch to wash the mud away and was doing pretty good when Tommy came around the corner. Doctor Hill was trying to keep pace with the sheriff to tell him to calm down.

"Stay out of this Doctor." Tommy said.

The doctor backed off.

Mary came out to stand beside the doctor. She was a knowing woman about people. She saw in Tommy a gentle man who would be pushed only so far before he exploded.

"Someone has made the sheriff mad." She told the doctor. "I fell sorry for who ever it was."

Tommy stood beside Aulding. Aulding wiped blood away from his mouth and mud from his suit. He turned on the sheriff to speak.

"You are breaking the law. I will have your badge for..." Aulding never finished the sentence.

Tommy knocked him back into the mud puddle. Aulding jumped to his feet only to fall again as he slipped on the wet dirt. Tommy leaped off the porch and picked Aulding up by his coat lapels.

"What do you want?" Aulding screamed in Tommy's face.

"You asked the right question. Let's see how you do with answers." Tommy said.

"I want the name of the man who shot my deputy and the names of those who hired him." Tommy added.

"I cannot tell you that. They would kill me." Aulding said.

Tommy knocked him out of the mud puddle and down the small embankment onto the sidewalk. Aulding was in good shape but he got up more slowly this time. Tommy walked toward him. Aulding backed away down the sidewalk. He started to run but lost his footing. Tommy took his time catching up to him. Tommy stripped a slender limb from one of the hotel hedges. He pushed the leaves off with one hand. As Aulding tried to turn away, Tommy brought the limb across his legs. Aulding jumped and was struck again and again. The story would be told for years to come of how the Sheriff of Hatsworth hickory whipped a criminal up and down the street as a means of interrogation.

Finally, Aulding's spirit was broken. He sat in the middle of the street crying like a child. He gave Tommy the names of the man who killed the deputy and the owner of the business in the city that served as their headquarters in the south.

"I begged them not to do it." Aulding sobbed. "I said it would just stir you up more. I begged them."

"I believe you did. I will not lock you up but stay in town. If I come back and you are gone, I will hunt you down. You understand?" Sheriff Bookmark asked.

"Yes. I understand. But what will I do? I just lost my job." Aulding asked.

"Come with me. I will try to help you out." Tommy ordered.

Aulding obeyed and walked to the hotel behind Tommy. He stood quietly as the sheriff talked to Doctor Hill.

"The doctor says you can wash dishes to pay for your food and room." Tommy told Aulding.

"Wash dishes?" The question burst from Aulding's mouth.

Tommy raised the limb to warn Aulding that it was still there.

"Say thank you to the good doctor." Tommy ordered.

"Thank you doctor." Aulding obeyed.

"You can go clean up and change into some work clothes Mister Aulding." Doctor Hill said.

Aulding looked at Tommy. Tommy nodded his approval and Aulding took off up the stairs.

"You were rough on him." The doctor said.

"I feel bad about that but sometimes unpleasant things are necessary. If he gives you trouble, just tell Sparky." Tommy

said.

"He will behave. You broke him good." The doctor said a little irritated at seeing a man's spirit broken so thoroughly.

"He should be glad that I am a God-fearing man or he would be in the morgue." Tommy said as he went to his car.

Tommy sat down in his car to calm down. Suddenly, he got out of the car and returned to the hotel.

"I need Aulding for a couple of days. I will send him back when I am finished with him." Tommy told Doctor Hill.

Tommy went up the stairs two steps at a time and walked toward Aulding's room. Miss Alice saw him pass and called to him. He turned and entered her room.

"Yes, Miss Alice." Tommy said.

"I heard about all the ruckus. I can imagine what you plan to do now. Just remember who you are. Do not become the kind of men you are hunting." Alice told him.

Tommy thought the advice over thoroughly before saying anything.

"You are a woman of remarkable insight. Thank you for reminding me. Please pray for my family while I am gone." He said.

"Oh, I have been doing that for some time now. You, as well. Just do not forget to reload. God does not reward stupidity." She said.

Tommy laughed as he left the room. She had a way of getting to the point in a hurry. He stopped at the door of Aulding's room then opened the door and walked in without knocking. He caught Aulding in the process of putting his pants on. Aulding tried to hurry but fell on the floor, still holding his pants with one foot in a leg of the pants.

"Bookmark, you have a way of scaring a man half to death." Aulding said.

"It is your conscience, Aulding, I will help you redeem yourself for all the drunks you have helped create." Tommy

said.

He, of course, knew from church that Aulding could in no way redeem himself but it was a language the criminal understood.

"I thought of something I would like for you to do for me if you do not mind." Tommy said.

"Do I have a choice?" Aulding asked.

"What do you think?" Tommy began with a question then continued. "I want you to haul one last load of shine to the city. You will pick it up as usual and deliver it to your usual place. I want you to do everything just as you always do it. If you stopped off anyplace in the past, do so on this trip. Consider it your last fling. You will then return to Hatsworth and resume your job with Doctor Hill. Do you understand?" Tommy asked.

"Yes. I understand." Aulding answered.

"When is your next normal delivery?" Tommy asked.

"Tonight." He replied.

"Then you better get on a fresh suit. You have some driving to do. You even have time to take a bath. You smell awful." Tommy said.

"I need to get my legs doctored up too. You beat the hide off both of them." Aulding moaned.

"Get it done. I will follow you into the city. Wait outside of town. I will be along." Tommy said.

Tommy used the time to run home for supper and surprise Marsha. He hated goodbyes but he could not resist seeing her one more time before he left. It would be several hours before Aulding completed his pickups.

Chapter

14

Aulding waited, as he was told to do, outside of town. Tommy arrived feeling good and with a full stomach. Aulding had missed supper and was a little grumpy. Tommy ignored him and told him to go ahead and take off. Tommy removed his sheriff's badge from his coat and put his revenue badge and identification inside his coat pocket. They drove for an hour and a half until they arrived at the farmer's market just south of the city.

Tommy watched as Aulding made his delivery. He prowled through the vegetables making comments about the quality and asking for the price. He appeared every bit the farmer he was. He could see Aulding conferring with people a few docks down from where he was 'shopping'. The quart jars were placed in a stack of honey with some of the honey stacked on top to hid it. No doubt it would be transported as honey in disguise.

Aulding was speaking to a tall man with a mustache. His name was Frank Kidd. Another man stood by, his name was Pacheco Deno. He was short, fat and bald. They would have been a comical looking pair had it not been for their line of work and the shotguns they kept hid in their little office. They also had revolvers, in holsters under their coats.

Tommy's six sense of danger warned him. He put an extra

cylinder of ammo in his coat pocket in easy reach. He reached into the top of his boot and pulled out a second pistol. He placed it at the small of his back. His ammunition was interchangeable with either weapon.

Aulding took his money and set off for his local hangout, a local bar. They served meals with the booze which sounded good to Aulding, at the moment. The men asked him about the killing of the deputy before he jumped off the dock.

"I told them it was a bad idea." Tommy heard him say as he moved closer to the men.

"You got one less lawman to worry about. Stop your moaning." Deno told him.

"You do not know that sheriff up there. He has a nasty way about him when he gets mad. The last time I saw him he was really upset. He has walked into more bullets than our whole organization put together. The people up north in Hatsworth think he won the war all by himself. He is still breathing by the way." Aulding said. It almost sounded as if he was proud of his nemesis. Tommy heard the exchange and smiled.

"Well, send him on down here. We got some more bullets for him to dodge." Kidd said patting his pistol.

Aulding turned toward his car. "Be careful what you wish for."

"What was that?" Deno asked his back.

Aulding kept walking as if he did not hear the question. He even smiled a little after he got his car turned away from the two men. He had seen Tommy coming up between the stacks of honey and moonshine.

"Hello boys." Tommy said looking over the barrel of his revolver. "I am the Sheriff of Hatsworth and recently appointed federal agent. Please drop your weapons on the floor."

"Where is your army?" Kidd asked.

"Looking at you." Tommy said indicating the revolver with a slight tilt of the weapon.

The two men split up. One ran into the office and came up with a shotgun. The other ran under some hanging hams and behind some empty wooden pallets. Tommy took cover behind the honey and illegal whiskey. Deno, the one under the hams, was trying to flank Tommy to get a clear shot without hitting the whiskey. Tommy saw the move and changed his position. He shot the string holding one of the smoked hams. It hit its mark landing on Deno's head. He went down.

Kidd gave up on saving the whiskey and fired the shotgun in Tommy's direction. He succeeded only in spilling honey and whiskey all over the dock. Tommy made his way further back past the stacks of jars. He was in no hurry. He darted unobserved behind the further end of the small office. He stepped on some empty pallets and pulled himself to the top of the office. He turned his head toward the dock and told Kidd to put down the shotgun. Kidd was not sure of the direction but shot in Tommy's general direction bringing down bits of the building ceiling on him.

"You are under arrest for trafficking in illegal whiskey." Tommy said officially.

"In your dreams cop." Kidd said as he fired at the top of the office. He emptied the shotgun and reached for his revolver. Tommy had counted the shots and hoped there was not an extra round in the weapon. He raised up enough to get a clear shot and gave one more warning. He was in clear sight of Kidd. Kidd started to raise the pistol and Tommy shot him. He immediately dropped from the roof of the small office and retrieved the weapons. He found the other shotgun in the office and took it as well. Then, he went to where the fallen Deno was. He was trying to get up looking around dumbly for the pistol he had dropped. His eyes had trouble focusing.

Tommy leveled the shotgun he had gotten from the office at the man. "Like I told your friend, you are under arrest."

Deno's pistol had fallen and slid under some old cardboard. Tommy spotted it and picked it up. Despair filed the countenance of the outlaw. Without his pistol, he was just a short, fat man. He was vulnerable and he knew it. Tommy directed the nervous man back to the office. There he handed him a card with the local revenue department phone number on it.

"Call these people and tell them you found some moonshine and two dead bodies on the dock at the farmers market." Tommy told him.

"There is just one dead body." The man said stupidly.

"There will be two by the time they get here." Tommy told him raising the shotgun a little.

"You can't just shot me down." The man protested.

"I can. I want to know where the man is who killed my deputy. His name is Manson Smog." Tommy told him.

"He is the boss's personal bodyguard. You must be crazy." Deno said.

"The Germans thought so. Where is Smog?" He asked again as he stuck the barrel of the shotgun against Deno's chest.

The man began to sweat. He crossed his legs out of fear. When he told Tommy what he wanted to know, it was in a high pitched voice. Tears rolled down his face as he talked.

The local federal agents came screeching into the market yard with sirens blasting. Men poured from their cars. Tommy and Deno were surrounded in seconds. The agents did not know who to subdue. Deno looked like a local but a big man they did not know was holding the shotgun.

"Drop the weapon." One yelled.

"Of course, officer." Tommy said.

"Who are you?" Another asked.

"Special Agent for your department. My identification is in my pocket." Tommy said.

An officer reached into Tommy's pocket and pulled out his sheriff's badge. "This is a sheriff's badge, you are out of your jurisdiction." He said.

"Wrong pocket, officer. Check the other one." Tommy said.

The officer did and came out with the correct badge and picture of Tommy.

"So, you are THAT sheriff." He said.

"I guess so." Tommy said. "You will find stacks of illegal whiskey, moonshine to be precise, over there. It is mixed in with the honey. The deliveryman got away."

"Did you get any information out of this one?" The agent asked indicating Deno.

"No. He was too afraid to talk much. He may need a change of clothes." Tommy said.

Deno looked at him questioningly. Tommy winked at him. Deno then realized that the sheriff/agent was not going to share his deputy's killer with anyone. Aulding was right.

Sparky was busy back at the farm and with his sheriff duties. Today he was building a gate for the one road leading to the farm. He spent his own money to purchase some steel cable. He cut hickory trees and stripped the bark from them. When the job was done, he had a gate that could be easily swung by a child but, he hoped, would stop unwelcome visitors. Visitors would have to blow their horn or yell so someone could open the gate for them. The gate was just on the other side of the creek from the house. Mister McNeil thought it was a good idea. The creek would stop any road vehicle from bypassing the gate. The idea gave him a little more liberty to do the work needed around the farm. He went down to the Brown's to hire the boys to work on the fence. They turned out to be good at stringing the barbed wire. Mister McNeil had recommended six strands of wire to keep the calves from crawling through. The post were placed eight feet apart. A strong bull could run through the fence, when it was finished, but it was not likely that he would try.

Mister McNeil worked on turning the stalks from the previous crop back into the earth to enrich the soil. He too had a crop of potatoes to dig and take to market. The money from this sell would go toward money for Christmas. Christmas included those in the community who were less able to provide for their children. They had decided, this year, to pool their resources at the church where the needy could pickup something for the holiday.

Marsha and Mrs. McNeil worked in the potato field picking up potatoes and putting them into baskets. Mister McNeil would pick them up in the wagon, at the end of the day. He did not want them carrying the full baskets to the end of the rows. They also had a patch of turnips that were ready to harvest. Some, they would store, some would be sold in town. It took all the pieces of the farm puzzle to keep the place running at a profit. There would not be as much to do when real cold weather came but still they would work until time brought along the spring. The hogs would be slaughtered when the ground froze and the hams smoked slowly in the smokehouse. Sausage would be ground and canned. Lard would be made in the big wash pots and the skins chopped, boiled, salted down and dried. There might be time for hunting which would supplement their meat supply and offer some variety. Deer meat prepared correctly could be a special treat in the cold winter months.

Sparky learned every day. His education followed two channels. One on the farm where there was always something new to learn and remember. Then, the sheriff job where he dealt with local citizens who were mostly friendly and gentle, while watching for the criminal elements from out of town. He found support from most of the people he encountered. They understood the job he had to do and the danger that was ever present for him when he carried a badge. He also

145

had opportunity to meet Betty on his trips to get the boys and take them home. He usually let them sleep on the McNeil farm overnight, so he could take them home every other night, thus saving a lot of valuable time.

Betty reacted to Sparky with maturity and grace. Mrs. Brown allowed her to skip some of her chores so she could spend some time with Sparky when he came to bring the boys home. She would sit pertly in the living room while her father and Sparky talked about the latest events. Then her father would make a discreet exit to do some chore he suddenly thought of to do. It gave Sparky and Betty time to talk with interruptions only from Lilly who was uncontrollably naughty when her sister had a 'date'. Lilly often thought of things to ask her sister about. Sometimes she overheard part of a conversation and would blurt out her opinion. Sparky found it very humorous. Betty found it very annoying. She even found it annoying when Sparky laughed at Lilly's antics.

Their relationship grew in a pure and beautiful way. They were eventually allowed to take walks to the river and along the roads at the end of the fields. Betty forgot her crush on Tommy and had eyes only for the strong young man who seemed wiser than his years. A force drew them to each other. At some unknown point, they accepted, without words, that they could never again be happy alone. Betty learned not to be threatened by Lilly and even invited her along on some of their walks. Betty's childhood was over and her whole life now pointed to one man and their future together. Sparky began to make plans of his own. They would need a house to live in. He had saved most of his money from the military service and his two jobs. He got Betty to talk about the kind of house she wanted and so he began to draw up the plans. He took her to see Tommy and Marsha's house. He watched as her eyes light up.

"It is beautiful and perfect but it must have cost a lot." Betty said.

"We will manage." Sparky said.

Tommy got on a bus for Charlotte. There was a packing company there he wanted to visit, a man he must see. Deno had given him the name of the owner, one Boss Lipston of Lipston Produce and Packaging. Tommy arrived in the evening hours and went straight to the local agency to check out a car to use while he was there. He staked out the packaging plant until he spotted the man Deno had described. He was not a young man but neither was he old and decrepit. His face was hard and lined from years of anger and hate. He wore an expensive suit and drove a shiny car with a special paint job. The man lived high. Tommy watched the man leave after the first day of surveillance. A second car pulled out and followed Boss. Four men watched from the vehicle for any threats to their boss. They were apparently body guards. Tommy decided that Boss Lipston must have a lot of enemies. For a week Tommy watched the man. He kept a safe distance and lost him a couple of times. By the end of two weeks however, he had worked out the man's routine.

Boss liked to eat well, as evidenced by his size. He threw money around freely. The ladies liked this part and were very affectionate to Boss when he was in places of business.

There was a back room card game on Friday nights. Tommy sat in the bar on the second Friday night drinking ginger ale. He appeared to be just another business man as he sat on the bar stool with his tie loosened and sitting bent over his drink. He rubbed his head as if he had not had a good week. Had anyone noticed his calloused hands, they would have known that he was not the office type. The four goons were near Boss all the time. They even worked shifts to protect him while he slept. He would be a hard man to get to.

"Divide and conquer." Tommy thought aloud.

"What did you say?" The bartender said.

"Oh, I've been reading a war story. I must have been talking to myself."

"You want another drink?" The bartender inquired.

"No. I was just leaving." Tommy said.

Tommy went to the local agency and showing his identification, he asked for the mug shots of known criminals with connection to organized crime. He flipped through books of pictures late into the night. He found a picture of two of the bodyguards. He took them to another desk to check for outstanding warrants. Both had out of state warrants pending. Tommy arranged for the local police to pick them up at the bar. The cops, knowing the situation, went in force to avoid a shot out. The two bodyguards did not resist figuring that their boss's lawyer would have them out before daylight. Tommy arranged for them to be extradited before they could make any phone calls. He sent them to the states where the warrants were outstanding. Boss would replace them but not tonight.

Tommy went to see the city police chief. He told the man what he was up against.

"Sure I can get them on a broken headlight or something. I am sure the passenger will resist or interfere with the performance of an officer doing his lawful duty." The police chief said.

"Good. Shuffle them around town for a day or two to keep them away from their lawyer." Tommy said.

"Easy enough. We do have some overcrowding problems." The chief laughed. "You sure know how to stir up a can of worms."

"I just want to put away a couple of snakes." Tommy said.

Tommy followed Boss home from his business the next night. Two police cars swooped past him and pulled over the car with the two bodyguards inside. There was a little commotion but it ended with the two in handcuffs. Boss was unaware of the action. Tommy closed in on him and stopped at a distance from the house. Boss went inside assuming that

his guards would watch through the night. He called his
lawyer about the first two bodyguards and left it in his hands
to get them free. Stuff like this happened all the time in his
business which was why he spread around a lot of money.
Boss went upstairs and climbed into his bed, already warmed
by a woman whose name had slipped his mind. She stirred
but did not awaken. Boss was tired anyway and so pulled up
his covers to his ears and turned off the lamb.

He was fast asleep when the sheets were ripped away from
him. A bright flashlight blinded his eyes from seeing who was
holding it. The barrel of a pistol pushed against his neck
under his chin. He tried to move and heard the hammer being
pulled back. He got suddenly still, aware that he was only a
slight squeeze from death.

"What do you want?" Boss asked the unknown assailant.

"Justice." Tommy said roughly pushing the pistol harder.

The woman awoke and screamed a little before Boss
quieted her. "Shut your mouth. You want to get me shot."

She climbed out of bed with a sheet pulled to her front and
backed into a chair by the window. She was deathly afraid
and wept uncontrollably.

"Do not cry." Tommy said. "You are not on my list."

She quieted and strained to see the man behind the voice.

"What do you want?" Boss asked again.

"Justice." Tommy repeated.

"You said that. What is this all about? What justice?" Boss
said.

"You ordered my deputy killed." Tommy said.

"You're that crazy sheriff from down in Georgia. You have
overextended yourself this time." Boss said.

"I am also a federal agent. I am taking you in on suspicion
of trafficking in illegal whiskey." Tommy informed him.

"You will never get out of this house alive." Boss said.

"We shall see. Get dressed. You can dress in the other
room young lady. Boss will let you borrow his car to go home.

Won't you Boss?" Tommy said, again pushing on the revolver.

"Sure. Sure. The keys are on the counter downstairs." He said.

"Young lady." Tommy stopped her with his voice. "Go straight home and do not call anyone. Just go home and be glad to be alive."

"Yes sir." She said as she left the room adjusting the sheet over herself.

"Your crazy." Boss said.

"So, be careful and don't set me off." Tommy said motioning for him to get dressed.

Outside Boss looked around for his bodyguards and seemed to get angry when he could not spot them. Tommy put the man in his car and drove him to the police station.

Tommy made a phone call and had someone wake up a judge to get a search warrant for Lipston Produce and Packaging. He went there to wait for the searchers and the warrant to arrive. The warrant arrived soon enough. Tommy led the searchers to the crates of honey where he knew they would find quarts of moonshine as well. It was the paperwork in Boss' office that provided the sweetest rewards. He had a list of his distributors and a ledger of payoffs to local officials. Boss' personal phone directory would be fodder for months of investigation by the agency.

Tommy left the search to the professionals and went to the jail to talk to Lipston. A revenue agent met him before he went in to see the prisoner.

"Boss made a phone call to his lawyer. We listened on an extension. You should hear what he had to say." The agent said.

Tommy read the transcript of the call. Lipston was ordering his lawyer to get busy getting him out of jail. He also made reference to bringing in some fresh men to fill the gaps left by the arrests. One last comment left Tommy deeply afraid.

"Tell Smog to go to the source." Boss said on the transcript.

Tommy rolled the statement over and over in his mind. He could not make sense of the remark. He got clearance to go in to see Lipston. The man did not act like someone who was facing prison time. He acted smug and confident. Apparently, he had been in the same situation on other occasions.

"Your day has come Boss. You may as well tell me where Smog is. He is the main one I want." Tommy said in a calm voice.

"You will know soon enough, Sheriff, where Smog is." Boss said. "You are in WAY over your head. Since you are involved, you will pay the same as others, who have crossed me."

Tommy left the jail. He went to the local agency and talked to the agent-in-charge.

"What does Lipston mean when he says 'I will pay the same as others who have crossed me?'" Tommy asked.

"You should get home Sheriff. Organized Crime boss's are notorious for killing the families of those who interfere in their business. That is why it is so hard to crack down on them. We cannot protect our families all the time." The agent-in-charge told him.

Realization sweep over Tommy.

"I have to get home." Tommy said.

"Take my car." The agent told him. "It is the fastest one in the area. I built the motor myself."

He went to the car and fired up the big engine. The car shook with the roar of the motor. Apparently, the agent had built the car to catch whiskey runners. He pointed the car toward home and mashed the accelerator down. The car responded, with plenty of power left. He rolled through the night. In one town, he picked up a local cop who turned on his lights and gave chase. Tommy did not have time to stop to explain. He mashed the accelerator further down. It seemed to make the engine happy. The car gained speed leaving the police car in the distance. Somewhere Smog would be making his way to the farm, perhaps to kill his family in retaliation for the arrest of Boss Lipston. He had to get there first.

Smog was not in Charlotte. As a matter-of-fact, Aulding had seen him in the Atlanta and avoided him. Smog was sitting in the bar when the phone call came from the lawyer. He smiled a wicked smile. If Smog had any redeeming qualities, they were well hidden and calloused over from years of killing. He liked the jobs that no one else would do. He had come to enjoy the screams of the women and the fear they showed. Children were still a little difficult for him but he managed.

Manson Smog drove down to the gate Sparky had erected. He honked his horn and waited for Mister McNeil to walk down. Smog got out and announced that he was selling insurance. He put in a barrel laugh where ever it seemed appropriate. He could not help but notice the double-barrel shotgun Mister McNeil carried. Sparky was on duty until midnight at the sheriff's office.

"Mister Smog, it is a little late to be making sells calls on farmers. We usually get to bed early and get up before the sun." Mister McNeil said.

"I could work out a plan and come back during the day. That way, I would not take up much of your time. How many are in your family?" Smog asked leaning on the gate with one huge arm.

"There is just me and the wife. My daughter and her husband have one child. Perhaps, you could come by on Saturday. We slow down a little then." Mister McNeil said.

Smog made a mental note of the family members. Mister McNeil had not mentioned that Sparky lived on the farm. It was a good thing. Mister McNeil only thought that the policy would cover blood kin and not their adopted friend. By his reasoning, he had left Smog with an incomplete picture, quiet

by accident. Smog backed up the drive until he found a place
to turn around. He took his time driving around the farm.
The fence was coming along nicely. The post were all in and
much of the wire had been strung. The gate was the only
place he could drive his car. If he had brought wire cutters,
he could have used one of the field roads. He made a mental
note to include cutters in the store of equipment he kept in
the car. He found a place on the back side of the farm to pull
off the road, amongst some trees, to wait. While he waited, he
smoked a cigar creating a cloud of smoke around himself and
the car. The name Smog fit him perfectly. Where ever he
went he smoked up his own personal smog.

Smog checked his weapons while he waited. He preferred
to catch everyone asleep. The surprise added to his
excitement. He was not just a man who had a dirty job to do.
The job was dirty, indeed, but he relished what he did. He
ran his hands over the sawed-off shotgun with the short
stock, which he carried under his great overcoat. He carried
two revolvers on his belt. He also carried a 'billy' club in his
hip pocket. While he waited, he filled his pockets with extra
ammunition. It was much more than he needed but it was his
habit to carry enough to fight his own war, if necessary.

Unseen by Smog, Sparky finished his shift and drove down
the drive to the farm houses. He found the hidden key near
the gate and let himself in. He blinked his lights three times
after he shut the gate for the benefit of anyone he may have
awakened. He drove to the barn and parked his car inside the
hallway, where he had slept since Tommy left. He knew he
was trusted but he did not want to give way to any gossip.
Marsha objected at first but then understood. She did not
think in those channels of thought, so Sparky had to almost
spell it out for her. She was embarrassed when she realized
that people might think she and Sparky would do anything
while her husband was away.

Mister McNeil had awakened and watched from the

window as Sparky gave the signal with his lights. Marsha awoke as well. Thomas stirred and she sat in the darkness at the window feeding him as she watched lightening in the distance. Sparky turned off the car and went to the storage room where he had made himself a room to sleep in. It was comfortable and he enjoyed being there, especially, when it rained on the tin roof. The moisture filled air, drifting into the little room, felt good. He pulled his quilt to his shoulders and settled in for the night. Lying on his back looking up at the loft above, his thoughts went to Betty, as they often did during the day and night. Their love had grown on a daily basis. Plans for marriage had been a natural part of their budding relationship. It was one thing he wanted to do the right way. He tried to do right in all things but his marriage had to be right for sure. He closed his eyes and fell into a deep sleep.

Tommy turned north near the city and was on the last leg of his journey. He mashed the accelerator pedal further down. The powerful engine seemed to love the action and responded with more speed.

First there came the wind whipping the trees around like twigs. The tops circling around in an unwilling dance. Then the rain came, slanting at first, then straight down in large drops. More wind, this time laying the trees half over from west to east. A bolt of lightening connected the clouds to the earth below. Thunder seemed to shake the rain drops from the clouds causing streams to run in every direction from high to low ground.

Mrs. McNeil shuddered in her sleep and Mister McNeil reached for her and pulled her closer. Marsha held and rocked Thomas in the big chair. He sleep as long as she held him but if she laid him in his bed, he would cry when the thunder came. Sparky awoke and lay in his bed listening to the thunder. Tommy turned on his windshield wipers and had to slow down because of the water on the road. Smog sat in his car smoking a cigar and drinking from a bottle he had brought along. He laughed aloud when the lightening danced on the wet earth and climbed up a tree near him. "What a great night!" He exclaimed to himself.

He fired up his engine and drove around the farm to the driveway of the farmhouses. Before he turned into the drive, he turned off his headlights. He reached under the dash and flipped a switch for his taillights so they would not come on when he braked. It was an old moonshiner's trick. They would pull off the road when the law pursued and wait for them to pass. Then they would proceed down the road as if nothing had happened.

Smog gained speed to ram the gate.

Another bolt of lightening and then thunder that shook the houses and barns on their foundations. The loud clap of thunder came as Smog made contact with the gate. He thought to crash through and drive to the house but the gate only gave on one side. Smog's car hung in the gate as it swung to one side. The back of the car swung around and went off the bridge into the creek. Smog cursed that he had not seen how the gate was rigged. He saw that it was built well but did not notice that it was built to give way just enough to throw, anyone ramming it, off the road. It was a genius of an idea that Smog could appreciate if he were not soaking wet and climbing out of his wrecked car. He would have to steal a car to flee the scene.

The storm made the night much darker. Thunder rumbled in a torrent of seeming anger. Water ran in sheets from rooftops on the farm. It grew quiet for a moment and the storm seemed to be over but the storm was not tired. It moved, ever so slowly to the east causing the earth to tremble under its power.

Sparky awoke thinking he had heard something unusual in the storm. The large clap of thunder had drowned out the noise of Smog crashing the gate. Sparky held his hand in front of his face and could not see it. He looked outside and saw only blackness.

The storm lingered over them seeming to work up energy to cross the mountain behind the houses. Sparky gazed into the darkness seeing only when the lightening flashed. The flashes let him see but caused the darkness to seem even darker to his eyes when it was over. Once he saw what looked like a bear wondering across the yard. It was not possible. The animals in the barn would have smelled the bear and alerted him. The lightening made things look different in the sudden flashes. He laid uneasily back on his bed.

Smog waited on the porch with his shotgun ready in his hand. A long rumble of thunder gave him his opportunity and he kicked the door in. The door jam splintered under his mighty kick. He stood in the doorway waiting for what he knew would happen. Mister McNeil came rushing into the kitchen carrying his shotgun but not in a position to shoot quickly. Smog was ready and pulled the trigger. The heavy shots stopped Mister McNeil in mid-stride and pushed him backward. He tried to raise his shotgun and another blast tore at his body sending him bleeding and dead to the floor.

The rain beat down hard on the roof tops. It muffled the screams of Mrs. McNeil as she rushed from her bedroom in her nightgown. She saw her husband in a flash of lightning and ran to him. She lifted his head and shoulders and tried to talk to his dead body hoping for some sign of life, all the time, hoping that she was still asleep and this was a terrible nightmare. Praying that this night was not happening. She looked around for what could have caused such an unspeakable thing. Smog stood in the doorway in his great overcoat enjoying the moment. Laughter rumbled up from his chest like the thunder rumbled in the clouds outside. Mrs. McNeil reached for her husband's shotgun but it would not move from the floor. It seemed to be nailed in place. Smog's big left foot stood on the barrel. She beat at the big leg of the monster standing over her.

"You've gotten your clothes all bloody." Smog said to her as he reached down and ripped her nightgown from her body.

She coward on the floor over her husband's body trying to hide her shame. Suddenly, she was heaved from the floor by her long beautiful hair. She always wore it down when she slept. Smog brought up the butt of the shotgun and slammed it into her abdomen. The air in her lungs came out in one agonizing gust. She felt her body sailing through the air. She landed partially on the bed, her feet dangling to the floor. Smog swaggered into the room taking off his big coat. She looked at him in horror. The scream that she held in her throat would not come out without the air she had lost from her lungs. She tried to breath but a piercing pain burned her lungs as if they were on fire.

Tommy drove through Hatsworth without letting up on the accelerator. He went by the church and breathed another prayer. One of many he had prayed on his way home. Sparky could not get back to sleep. He looked outside to see a light in the McNeil's bedroom. It was a strange sight this time of night but Sparky was not a nosey person. He figured a man could turn on his light in the middle of the night if he was pleased to do so. Just the same, he got dressed and walked outside. He strolled down the driveway and was almost on the bridge before he saw the car in the creek. Just as Sparky realized that something was terribly wrong, Tommy came down the drive like the devil, himself, was after him.

Smog was finished in the McNeil house. He did not shoot Mrs. McNeil. It would have been an act of mercy, if he had done so. He found that his mission was more successful if someone were left to tell the story. He made his way up the hill to where Marsha was still holding Thomas in the big chair. She could have doused in the chair, as she often did, but something told her to pray. She was sensitive to such things. Her feeling that there was a great need to pray overwhelmed her and she poured out her heart to God as she rocked her sleeping baby boy. She could not see in the darkness outside but there were times when she sensed movement on the farm. She saw the lights of Tommy's car just as the kitchen door crashed inward. She dropped Thomas on the soft bed and grabbed for the revolver on the table beside the bed.

"You check the McNeil house. I will check on Marsha." Tommy snapped.

"Yes sir." Sparky said, already in a dead run.

Tommy mounted the steps on the kitchen porch. The kitchen door was hanging on one hinge and obstructed his entry. He kicked the door into the kitchen and stepped on top of it. Smog was only a few steps ahead of him. He turned with the shotgun in hand and fired in Tommy's direction. Tommy dove to one side, rolled over and came to his feet. Smog was on top of him before he could bring his pistol level to fire. The butt of the shotgun struck Tommy on the side of the head sending him across the kitchen in a heap. His mind went black but a voice told him he had to get up again. Tommy stood to his feet, staggering against the table. Smog raised the shotgun to finish Tommy off. Tommy stood with blood streaming down his face and over his eyes. He wiped it away and tried to raise his pistol. It was so heavy. He must raise it before the monster in front of him could fire. He must kill him to protect Marsha even if he died in the process.

Tommy heard two loud blast from his pistol. In his fog, he had not remembered raising the weapon. The man-monster turned with the blow of the slugs hitting him. The shotgun he held went off into the ceiling then fell to the floor. The man's big right hand reached to his belt and clasped around a revolver. He drew the weapon and pointed it not at Tommy but toward the other room. Another blast of two shots shook the big man and he fell as he turned toward the kitchen door.

The fog cleared somewhat from Tommy's brain. He looked down at his pistol. It was still by his side. There was none of the familiar smell of gunpowder. He did not remember the slight kick he usually felt when he fired.

His thoughts returned to Marsha and he started toward the bedroom. As he did so, he saw Marsha standing in the doorway. She was beautiful with her hair about her shoulders, her nightgown emphasizing her exquisite figure. The pistol in her hands still pointed at the man on the floor. A trail of smoke escaped the barrel. Tommy had not fired after all. His lovely wife had saved his life.

He reached for her and took the pistol from her hand. She was trembling. Then her motherly instincts shook her from her fright. She turned from Tommy to run to the bedroom to check on Thomas. She feared, now, that he might have rolled off the bed. Such a small thing, it seemed, after what she had just done. Thomas sat up on the bed and waved cheerfully as she entered the room.

Tommy grabbed the beast of a man by his coat and dragged him outside. He would not be doing any more killing. Not tonight, not any night.

"Are you alright?" He asked Marsha. "I need to check on your parents and Sparky."

"Yes." She said clutching Thomas to her bosom.

Tommy ran to the McNeil house to find the kitchen door busted. He saw Mister McNeil's body sprawled in the next room. He called for Sparky but got no reply. He entered the bedroom announcing himself. Sparky sat on the bed holding Mrs. McNeil in his arms. He had covered her with a sheet and was rocking her back and forth on the edge of the bed. Tommy spoke to her but she could find no words in her tortured mind. Little sounds came from her throat. She pointed toward her husband and made other sounds that could not be called words.

"We need help." Tommy told Sparky.

He ran to tell Marsha to stay in the house and that he would be back in just a few minutes. He turned the big engine loose up the driveway and to Hatsworth. He told the preacher very quickly what had happened, then hurried back to his house to tell Marsha about her parents. She cried and could not stop crying but did not get hysterical.

"Mama will need me, as soon as someone comes to watch Thomas." She said.

"Someone will be here soon to help us." Tommy said.

Come they did. Brother Newton came first then Doctor Hill with Bertha his wife and Mary the cook. Mary went to watch Thomas for Marsha so she could tend to her mother. Doctor Hill and Bertha went to the McNeil house to see about Mrs. McNeil. When Tommy reentered the McNeil house, Sparky still sat rocking Mrs. McNeil back and forth on the bed. His face was stern but stained with tears. He would not turn her loose until Marsha came to his side. Sparky felt, inside, like he had failed them all. He was suppose to have protected them. He had promised.

Hands reached for Sparky as he left the house but he would not acknowledge them. Tommy followed him outside. Tommy placed his hand on Sparky's shoulder. Sparky flung it away and stepped off a few feet. Tommy gave him space.

"You did all you could do, Sparky. It would not have happened any different if I had been here." Tommy said.

"He raped her and killed her husband. He has destroyed her. She still breaths but he destroyed the lady." Sparky said. Then he broke. Tommy had never seen the man cry but he understood. Everyone has their limits. Tommy reached out both his arms to his friend and they hugged as brothers.

"I wish it had been me he killed." Sparky said.

"I feel the same, my friend, but we are left to put the pieces back together. It is hard to believe now, but life will go on and people need us." Tommy said.

"Yes sir." Sparky said as he straightened up and stepped back. As always, his friend brought him back to reality. He would not indulge in self pity again. That was what Tommy had taught him. It was not about him, it was about others. Others who needed him. Sparky walked off toward the creek bridge. He could be found there for many days checking

every car that came onto the property.

Chapter

15

Brother Newton came outside where Tommy stood watching his friend walk toward the creek.

"Any words of wisdom Preacher?" Tommy asked.

"Some things can be endured only through faith and prayer. Prayer prepares and prayer repairs."* Brother Newton said.

"Thank you, my friend. You are right on track." Tommy said.

Tommy walked back into the house to check on his wife. She had been strong through the whole thing. Later, she would cry over the happenings in their own house. Now, she was concerned only for her parents. Her daddy was in heaven, she knew, his pain had been over quickly. Her mother would suffer through the long days and nights ahead. The humiliation she had suffered in her own bedroom would have been enough to devastate her. The loss of her husband was more than she could bare. Mrs. McNeil did not wail or scream. She did not talk. She rocked back and forth on her bed. She did not seem to notice when Marsha washed and dressed her.

Mister McNeil's body was removed to the funeral home. Tommy took pictures of his body before he was cleaned up by the funeral director. He also took pictures of the doors and the mess in both houses. He took pictures of Smog as he lay in his kitchen and of the weapons used to commit the shootings. He took several shots of each and kept one copy for his personal use. The others would be used in criminal court.

Word spread quickly of the tragedy. People from the church brought food to the house and lingered in the yard talking in hushed tones. Each had to get past Sparky's post at the bridge. He stood in front of approaching cars until they stopped. Then, he walked to the driver's side to view those inside. He knew most of the people in the county and so passed most without question. Some, he would ask to get out of the car, so he could search it. People understood. Even if they had not, they would not have tried to get past this solemn young man. They could tell he was all business. The Brown's came to bring food. Betty was in the car and got out long enough to hug Sparky. She was the one person he would show his hurt to. A tear escaped one eye and she brushed it away. Few words were spoken. He knew she was feeling his hurt and sorrow.

It would not have been a good week for any criminal to try to break the law in Hatsworth. Laymen from the surrounding area converged on the town. They sat in their cars along the streets. They went for their meals at the hotel or someone brought them a plate from their home. Revenue agents from the city walked the streets in plain suits.

When it was time for the funeral, the governor was in line behind the family. The crime was not just against one family. It was a strike against law enforcement in general. Organized crime was trying to make a statement for them to keep their hands off their business. The solemn faces of the lawmen who came to the funeral showed that the plan had not worked. If anything, it had given them more resolve to do their job.

Mister McNeil was laid to rest a few spaces from where James Inkle, Jr. was buried. The dirt had settled on his grave and grass grew over it. A lone late purple flower smiled at those who looked in that direction. Mrs. McNeil stood at the grave site looking many years older. She had seemed to age even as one looked upon her face. She rocked gently against Marsha and Tommy. Sparky held little Thomas.

The preacher read from John chapter fourteen:

"Let not your heart be troubled: Ye believe in God, believe also in me. In my Father's house are many mansions: if it were not so, I would have told you. I go to prepare a place for you. And if I go and prepare a place for you. I will come again and receive you unto myself, that where I am there ye may be also."

Brother Newton raised his strong voice into the breeze that was blowing across the cemetery.

"We are not as the world who have no hope. We are believers in the promises of the God of the universe. He has said that we shall live again after death overtakes us. Death is but a stepping stone from this life to a much better life in glory. While our hearts are broken over the brutal way Mister McNeil left this life, no brutality can wipe away the hope in our hearts. As the martyrs burned at the stake for their faith, one man lifted his hand toward heaven. A friend had told him, "If you see Him, raise your hand." As the flames engulfed him the Christian raised his hand. Our hope is greater than the world's. While they seek to posses the best things in life. We already posses treasures beyond measure. Mister McNeil has gone to posses his many treasures."

Mrs. McNeil raised her head and looked at the preacher who was looking directly at her. She stopped rocking and looked down at the grave. Then, she raised her head toward heaven and let the tears flow down upon her black dress.

"That is right, Mrs. McNeil. He is not here in this grave. He is over yonder where "moth and rust does not corrupt." Brother Newton said.

Amens echoed around the assembly.

"The Bible says in Hebrews chapter 10 and verse 22a: 'Let us draw near with a true heart in full assurance of faith...'" Brother Newton quoted. "Amen."

Miss Alice raised herself up in her chair and sang in a soft voice a song by Fanny Crosby. "Blessed assurance, Jesus is mine. Oh, what a foretaste of joy divine." The crowd joined her in a proper ending to the service.

Mrs. McNeil walked to the preacher without assistance to thank him for the sermon.

"Have faith, Sister. You will see him again." He said.

"I know that I will. I just forgot for a moment." She said.

Tommy and Marsha took her by the arms and walked her to the car. Sparky followed with Thomas. He was as much of the family as anyone could be.

Uniformed lawmen put on their hats and saluted Mrs. McNeil as she passed to go to the car. On this occasion, they were armed. The family's guarantee that the funeral would not be interrupted.

Slowly the crowd dispersed to their places leaving the family to grieve. It is true of all of us when death comes. After people have been as nice as they can be and all the kind words are said, we must go home to face a life that will never be the same. Blessed are those who have the everlasting truth to lean on.

The doors had long been repaired and all signs of the killing had been cleaned up. Still, Mrs. McNeil hesitated when she walked to the place where her husband died. She entered the bedroom and dropped to her knees in sobbing prayer. They let her talk to the Master until she was finished.

"Now, where is my grandson." She said quiet suddenly.

"Sparky has him outside." Marsha said.

"I will get him." Tommy said.

Mrs. McNeil smiled for the first time since that night. She smiled at her daughter, then her grandson. She took him in her arms and sat at the kitchen table with him in front of her on the table.

Tommy and Marsha walked out to stand on the kitchen porch.

"He restoreth my soul." Tommy quoted the line from Psalm twenty-three.

Sparky had been standing in the yard. He turned away when Tommy and Marsha hugged.

"You should go see Betty." Tommy said. "I am sure she would like to see you."

"Will you be alright?" Sparky asked.

"We will be alright." Tommy said. "Go."

Sparky rushed to his car and was gone. He would not have mentioned it himself but he had longed to see Betty. He knew she would understand what he was feeling. He knew that just being near her would take away some of the pain he felt.

She was waiting on the front porch when he slid to a stop and ran to her. He held her for a long time. Mister and Mrs. Brown did not tell them that they were breaking the rules. It was not a time for rules. It was a time for healing.

They walked along the end of the fields down toward the swimming hole. Lilly watched them from the window but did not ask to go with them.

Tommy walked into the jail where Boss Lipston was being held. The man had a shelf lined with books. Newspapers were stacked to one side. He was being taken care of very well. Lipston smiled when Tommy entered the cell. The deputy who let him in stopped outside the door to wait.

"Could you give us some privacy?" Tommy asked the deputy.

Reluctantly the deputy walked to the end of the cell row.

Tommy sat down on the opposite bunk from Lipston. He looked at the smiling face and did not speak. He reached inside his jacket pocket and pulled out the pictures he had taken of the tragedy at the farm. He laid them on the table with the pictures facing Lipston. Slowly, one-by-one, he laid out the story in pictures. Lipston's smile disappeared.

"I told you that you were in over your head Sheriff."
Lipston said.

Tommy pulled out one last picture and laid it on the table.
It showed Manson Smog, the tough guy of organized crime,
laying in a pool of his own blood.

"I know nothing about this horrible incident." Lipston said
with a sneer.

"I am not here for your denial." Tommy began. "I am here
to give you a choice. You can confess to conspiracy to commit
murder and your lawyers part in the affair, or you can pull
some lawyer trick and walk free. In the last instance, you will
be facing me, personally. I believe in justice Mister Lipston
whether administered by the system or by my personal
hand."

"You cannot threaten me. You are an officer of the law."
Lipston blurted.

"I am making you a promise. You will face justice for your
crimes. The only choice you have is by whose hands justice is
rendered. What is your answer?" Tommy asked.

"I want to talk to my lawyer." Lipston said.

"Then, our conversation is over." Tommy said.

"Deputy, let me out of here." Tommy yelled to the jailer.

The door to the cell slammed with finality. Boss thought
fast. He tumbled the statements the sheriff said around in his
head. The sheriff had not raised his voice. He simple stated
the alternatives as if there were no other choices. Up until
that moment, Boss had only considered freedom as a choice.
Now, it did not seem like such a good choice. He had no desire
to face the sheriff, alone on the street or in his home. It would
be no life at all to walk through life jumping at every
slammed door or dog barking.

"Wait! Wait!" Lipston yelled at Tommy.

Tommy walked slowly back to the cell, tired of the whole
thing.

"I will sign what ever you want me to sign." Lipston said.

Tommy did not answer him but turned to the deputy.

"You heard him Deputy. He wants to confess. Get someone in here to take his statement. Make sure you witness the process. He has something to say about his lawyer. Get that on a separate document. I will go have some coffee and return in a half hour to read the statements." Tommy ordered.

The deputy did not work for Tommy but complied with the orders. Something had turned Lipston from arrogant to cooperative in less than five minutes. The deputy wanted no part of that side of the sheriff.

"Right away Sheriff." He said.

"Thanks." Tommy said as he walked toward the door to go across the street to get his coffee.

The prosecutor looked over the statements and agreed that they were sufficient to convict Boss Lipston and his lawyer.

Tommy headed home. It was over.

Chapter

16

A different kind of enemy struck Hatsworth and the surrounding area. The bole weevil ended the reign of cotton in the county. Some fought back with insecticides but there were environmental concerns about them. People were leaving the county to find work in the southeastern part of the state and as far away as Texas. Money was tight and the banks were making only the most secure loans. Sheriff Bookmark talked to Doctor Hill often. He seemed to have his finger on the pulse of the country. There was talk of some bad economic times to come. Brother Newton seemed to have special insight. He was preaching on faith a lot. He said the time to establish our faith was before the storm came, before the darkness came. Tommy had heard part of the sermon before but the preacher had refined and added to the message:

"Faith
Galatians 2:20
"I am crucified with Christ: nevertheless I live; yet not I but Christ liveth in me: and the life which I now live in the flesh I live by the <u>faith of the Son of God</u>, who loved me, and gave himself for me."

"Faith is something that is unique to the Christian way of life. It is manifest to some degree in other areas, such as, a child having faith in its parents. There is a peace to be found in the darkness. Faith must be established before the darkness comes. We must rest in the assurance that God will do what is right. It may not always be comfortable but it will always be right. There is a place where joy can be found when all the trimmings are gone and it is just you and God. The clutter of voices are gone and we can listen to Him speak to us."

Little did we know that the Lord through the preacher was preparing us for serious troubled times ahead. Such serious trouble, we had not experienced in our lifetime. The service closed with a hymn of faith and hope.

The regular Sunday dinner was spread and everyone gathered around to enjoy the food. The preacher stepped to the spot where he always prayed God's blessings on the food. Today was a little different. He had Mary Wilmington in tow. She shyly followed him to the spot and stood by his side. He placed his arm around her shoulders.

"Ladies and Gentlemen, we have an announcement to make. Mary and I will be married. You are all invited to attend the wedding, here at the church, in one month. A friend of mine from out of town will perform the ceremony and look after the preaching while we are on our honeymoon." Brother Newton announced in his hoarse preacher's voice.

A round of applause followed. Sparky reached for Betty's hand and was tempted to make an announcement of his own. He decided to not take any excitement from the preachers announcement. Soon, though, they would stand and make their wedding plans known.

Chapter

17

Thomas sweated over the shovel as he dug out the pit in the smokehouse. The pit would be used for storing potatoes. The procedure had been the same since Thomas was small. He had watched, many times, as his daddy dug out the pit each year. Then they would line the bottom with corn shucks and put on a layer of potatoes from their fields. Next, came another layer of corn shucks then potatoes until the pit was filled to about eight or ten inches from the top. In the cold months of winter, he would be sent out to dig up a layer of potatoes for the following week. It was not hard work for Thomas. He had grown up with a shovel, posthole diggers or some other farm instrument in his hands. His muscles were strong from splitting firewood and fencepost. He had earned the right to have his own cornfield, hayfield and a good number of cattle.

He walked to the door of the smokehouse to get some fresh air. He looked toward the yard where his mother and sister were making lard in the old wash pot. His sister, Laura, was a pretty girl of thirteen years. From a distance, Thomas had trouble distinguishing her from his mother. They were of the same build and their hair hung on their shoulders the same when they were working.

Laura bent to the task of stirring the hot liquid in the pot.

She used a long slim pole to avoid the hot grease and the heat from the fire. Presently, Marsha came out to dip out the cracklings. They would be good, cooked in cornbread. Once the cracklings were removed, Laura got to stop stirring and the grease was allowed to cool into lard. She went into the house to help her mother separate the cracklings and throw out those with some flaw or blemish. Laura remembered the great slabs of fat taken from their first hog slaughter of the year. She helped cut it into strips to put in the pot.

She, too, had grown to her present age working the farm. Many times, she had spent long hours turning the crank on the meat grinder to make sausage for canning. She knew how to put up canning without her mother being with her but they always worked together. What they canned depended on what was mature at the time. She spent long, hot hours boiling and peeling tomatoes to put with other vegetables for canned soup. It was a wonderful thing to open a jar of soup in the middle of winter and taste fresh vegetables. It was not her job but she had watched as her daddy and Thomas hung hams and shoulders in the smokehouse for smoking. Thomas and his daddy took turns checking the hickory wood fire. A small stove pipe in the roof of the building left the smell of hickory smoke in the yard for weeks.

Formal education was not neglected by her parents. Marsha ordered new books for them on a regular basis. She and Tommy taught them the basics very early in their life. They learned about the world around them from the books they read. Both children loved reading and did not look on it as work. Tommy and Marsha sat together in the evenings and read until bedtime. The children grew up watching them at first, then reading their own books. It was as natural for them as eating supper at the end of the day. Tommy was alert to their interest and always suggested reading material along those lines. The ever present newspapers were well read before they were put aside to start fires in the winter. Radio came to their home amid great excitement. They could now listen to news stories and some singing programs. Marsha was careful not to let the radio take the place of reading. The one hour they were allowed to listen after supper remained a special time for them.

Tommy stayed sheriff for three terms with his faithful friend by his side. Then Tommy recommended Sparky for the position of sheriff. Sparky won the next election with very little trouble. Tommy settled down to finally write the book he had started. They had come through the depression in pretty good shape, thus far. The farm provided most of what they needed and some to share with those less fortunate. The Brown's had a hard time of it, as sharecroppers. They were use to hard times, though, so they scraped for money to buy canning jars and lids to can everything they could grow. Sparky helped them as much as he could. He and Betty were married and now had two girls of their own. Lilly spotted a boy at church and he never had a chance. The boy had taken over his father's coal business in town. They were doing pretty good.

Tommy rocked in his chair on the porch. His hair was mostly silver now. He got up a little slower but his muscles still pushed against his shirt. He worked as he had always worked on the farm. He liked to walked to the fields in the spring and see where the tender corn stalks had pushed through the soil.

Today, however, was Sunday. They had attended church and were sitting around letting their dinner settle. He had allowed Thomas to read the first draft of his book, an account of the early years when he had come to town as a transient.

"Did all those things really happen? Did you really go to Charlotte after Boss Lipston?" Thomas asked anxiously.

"It is not something I talk about much, but yes. He had your grandfather killed. I had to see justice done." Tommy said.

"All this time, I thought you just broke up fights in town

and farmed." Thomas said.

"You do not have to do the things I did Thomas. We have been blessed to have peace in your lifetime. Duty must always come first. You will find your duty someday. If you never have to raise a weapon toward another human, you will be a blessed man." Tommy told his son earnestly.

"I understand. I would not want to kill anyone. I am just fascinated that I have been living with a hero all this time and did not know it." Thomas said.

"Some of the greatest heroes are in the cemetery. They gave all they had. I was just one man who wanted to come home. The Germans were in my way, so I did what I had to do. Just as you will when the time comes." Tommy said.

The conversation was necessary but Tommy had trouble talking about those days. He excused himself and walked down into the fields. His gray hair reflected the sunlight. Thomas watched him walk. He walked a little stiff but he had an easy way of moving. His head moved from side to side scanning every inch of his surroundings. It was a habit he could not break. He was seldom aware that he even did it.

Marsha walked out to the porch to stand beside her son.

"Where is your daddy going?" Marsha asked.

"I don't know. We were talking about his book and he just got up and left to go walking." Thomas said.

"He will be back soon. He carries a big load sometimes. He has had to take the lives of men. Your daddy is not a natural killer. He did what he had to do, but he remembers. You remember too, son. Never take another humans life lightly." Marsha said.

"I won't Mother." Thomas said. "Daddy is a good man. Isn't he?" Thomas said.

"He has carried his share of the load. He had to carry a gun but all he wanted to do was write when I met him. Now he just wants to write and farm. Yes. He is a good man." Marsha said.

Mrs. McNeil had moved into the house with Tommy and

Marsha. Most of her nightmares had stopped, but for years she woke up drenched with perspiration, as she relived that awful night. Sparky and Betty moved into the McNeil house. Tommy built another wing onto his and Marsha's house to accommodate the new additions to their household.

Laura was learning to play the piano. Marsha noticed her attraction to the church piano after the services. She would sit for a long time trying to pick out the notes. When someone else played, she would stand quietly watching the movements of their hands. Marsha saved for two years to get a piano for Laura. Laura declared that it was the best Christmas she would ever have. Today she sat at the piano playing some song she was making up as she went along. The music was soft and peaceful. Marsha thought it reflected the personality of her daughter. Tommy smiled to himself as he heard an occasional portion of the tune. Before long, he predicted, they would all gather around the piano and began to sing hymns. Laura did not read music but needed only a few words of a song to pick up the melody. The children were blessed with good singing voices like their mother and grandmother. When Tommy finally came back to the house, he heard them singing their hearts out even before he climbed the steps to the porch. It was a song Tommy and Laura had written together.

Are you lonely today, have you no friends to say?
  I love you and I really care.
Well, Jesus wants to stay,
  Close beside you all the way.
He won't leave you or lead you astray.

When others want to say
  Won't you please go away.
Jesus bids you come unto me -
  I want you around and I won't put you down.
I'll love you for all eternity.

For God so loved the world
  That He gave us His Son.
That whosoever believes in Him.
  Would never have to die, but live by His side.
Whosoever means you and me.

He loves you today, please don't turn Him away,
  When sorrow over you stays.
He loves you today
  Please don't turn him away.
Jesus loves you
  He'll be your best friend.

The song was titled <u>Jesus, Your Best Friend.</u> The children
had sung it in church and received a good response. It was a
song Laura wrote the music to while Tommy wrote the words
from his very soul, for Jesus had truly been his friend in
times of danger and loneliness. He let them finish the last
chorus before he went into the room, smiling the bright smile
they all loved. Marsha smiled back at him knowing that he
had once again dealt with the demons that often haunted him,

the guilt of being spared when his friends died, of those who sacrificed their lives for him, when he should have given his for them. The eyes of those who had died by his hand. He remembered the fear and terror in their eyes. He knew they were someone's children and he hated war when he thought of them. For now though, he went to sit in his chair and soon had a cup of coffee to drink while they sung another song.

"I have to go into town tomorrow so I will take some corn to be ground and bagged. I will drop it off at the grocer. We could use the cash." Tommy announced.

"May I go with you?" Thomas asked.

"Too much to do." Tommy said. "You know as well as I do what has to be done."

"Yes sir. It is the woodpile again for me." Thomas said.

"It is the sign of a man to know what is to be done and does it without being told to do it." Tommy said smiling.

"Some things I would prefer not to volunteer for." Thomas said.

"You sound like your Uncle Sparky. He always said he did not like to volunteer but was the first in line when I needed him. The old folks use to say 'You have to take the good with the bad.'" Tommy quoted.

"Yes sir." Thomas said.

"Pretend you thought of what to do. You should always demand more of yourself than anyone else demands of you." Tommy sermonized.

"Yes sir. Let's sing another song." Thomas said to Laura to get the attention off himself. He appreciated good advice but not all the attention he was getting from everyone.

Tommy finished his business in town and went to the hotel for dinner with Doctor Hill. Two of Mister Brown's youngsters were waiting tables for Mary. It was a flashback to the many years before when he had first sat at the big table. He remembered the soft perfume Marsha wore the first day he saw her. Doctor Hill moved a little slower but otherwise was still the same. Mary had picked up a limp from arthritis in one hip but she still looked after her girls, as she called them. Aulding was still working in the kitchen. He had become a valuable employee and could do most anything that needed to be done. Once he got over his pride, he found that he enjoyed being on the side of the law. He came out to Tommy and shook his hand.

"Thank you Sheriff for steering me right. I am attending church now and am the happiest I have ever been." Aulding said.

"Good for you Aulding. I am proud of you." Tommy said.

Aulding blushed tremendously and turned to go back in the kitchen.

"He has turned out to be a good man. He just needed some direction for his life and a lot of forgiveness." Doctor Hill said.

"We all need plenty of that." Tommy said.

Sparky and his wife were there with the children to eat the noon meal. It was easier for them than driving home to fix something. Mary liked fixing something special for the children. She really fussed over them when they came around.

"Old Sam retired from government service years ago but he still keeps up with everything." Doctor Hill volunteered.

"He was some kind of politician. I do not think anyone could have won an election against him." Tommy said.

"He mentioned your name in a speech." Doctor Hill said.

"Now, why would he do that?" Tommy asked.

"He said he would have to talk to you but thinks you would make a fine governor." Doctor Hill said.

Tommy came off his chair. He caught the edge of his plate and caused it to slam back on the table. He quickly apologized and sat back down. Mary had already come to the door to see what the racket was all about.

"I am a farmer not a politician." Tommy snorted.

"The country is coming out of a great depression and Germany is rattling its sabers again. The state needs a strong man in office while the country gets straightened out again." Doctor Hill argued.

"You would make a good governor." Sparky put in.

"I thought you were my friend." Tommy told him half joking.

"You may disappoint a lot of people." Doctor Hill said.

"Why do you say that?" Tommy asked.

Doctor Hill passed the newspaper down the line so Tommy could see the front page story. It had a picture of Tommy in his uniform and Old Sam when he was governor. There was a long write up about Tommy's war record and his fight with organized crime.

"Am I being drafted again?" Tommy asked.

"It looks like." Doctor Hill said. "Old Sam knew you would be more cooperative if he drummed up some publicity first."

"He wants me to feel guilty for disappointing all those people if I decide not to run. No wonder he was able to stay in office so long. He stacks the deck. If I played cards, I would never play with him. He cheats." Tommy said.

"Sounds like you know the man pretty good. I guess you better get on home and talk to your family. He will be coming to see you in a few days, if I know the old coot." Doctor Hill said.

Tommy had lost his appetite and headed for the door. Mary came out with a bag of goodies for her babies, as she still called Tommy's near grown children.

Tommy mumbled all the way home. "I am a farmer. All I want to do is farm and write my book. Who in his right mind would want to be governor."

His thoughts kept going back to his conversation with his son about duty being most important. Well, he hoped he could be governor with his foot in his mouth.

Back at the hotel, the conversation about the governorship continued.

"What do you think he will do Doctor?" Sparky asked.

"I think he will mumble all the way home. Then, I think his sense of duty will win him over. Old Sam thinks he will be a good governor. He said Tommy was the only man who ever scared him. He tells the story all the time about the soft spoken sheriff coming into his office and demanding that he be appointed a special agent. He just would not take no for an answer. He had executives opening doors for him. Tommy is a kind man who can get awful mean when he needs to." Doctor Hill speechulated.

Tommy did mumble but also did some praying. It seemed that his life was taking a course beyond his control. His desire, from the beginning, had been to write. Then, he had fallen in love with the life of a farmer. He loved to watch things grow and the whole cycle of things in general. Yet, circumstances far away seemed to draw him like a magnet. Some country decides to take over the world and he must take up arms to help stop them. Criminals try to invade his county and he is called upon to stop them. Now, it seemed he was being asked to do a task that was beyond his wildest dreams or nightmares of doing. Could he run a whole state?

"I guess I will find out soon enough." He said aloud to himself.

He pulled into the driveway of his home and was glad to see Marsha come to the door. She wiped her hands on her apron and tried to push back an unruly lock of hair. She squinted her eyes against the sinking sun, as Tommy walked up the trail to the front door where she was standing. He smelled the usual smells of the evening coming from the kitchen. She stood in the doorway until he got there and gave him a quick kiss before rushing back to her stove to check on supper. She had cornbread in the oven and it was already getting brown around the edges. Marsha hoped it did not stick today. Sometimes, part of the bottom crust would stick and pull the bottom of the bread cake off. It tasted the same but did not look as good on the table.

Tommy followed her into the kitchen and proceeded to aggravate her in general with his playfulness.

"You will cause me to let something burn!" She exclaimed.

He sat down at the table in front of the cup of coffee she had already poured for him. He had not realized that he was hungry but smelling the food cooking set his stomach to growling.

"They want me to run for governor." Tommy said offhandedly.

"Well, I know you will win." Marsha said while stirring some mashed potatoes. The statement sank in as she lifted the lid of another pot.

"Governor!" She exclaimed.

Thomas and Laura heard the exclamation all the way to the back porch where they were working on a project Marsha had assigned them. They dropped everything and dashed into the kitchen. Mrs. McNeil came from someplace to stand in the doorway.

"Governor!" The children repeated in unison.

"Sam Perks thinks I am the man for the times. I will probably get it with his backing." Tommy said.

"So, you have decided to run?" Marsha asked.

"Only if you all agree." Tommy said.

"Laura, please set the table. Thomas you may help her." Marsha said. "I respect what ever decision you make, Tommy, but what about your writing. I had hoped that you would finally get to do what YOU wanted to do." She added.

"Life is not about what I want. It is about doing the right thing. The depression has given unscrupulous men the opportunity to take advantage. Dictators are rising to power all over Europe and democracy is threatened." Tommy said.

"What does that have to do with being governor?" Thomas asked.

"Our nation will be tested. Our best people will be sent to

stop the aggression of evil empire builders. We must remain strong at home. The state governors will have to step up and take care of their respective states while the federal government deals with outside threats." Tommy explained.

"Will you be called up to serve again?" Mrs. McNeil asked.

"I do not think so, if I am governor. In a way, I would prefer to serve in uniform." Tommy said.

"Well, it sounds like it is going to happen. We may as well face it with our chin up. Supper is ready. Shall we eat?" Marsha said.

The conversation stopped while Tommy prayed God's blessings on the food and the world. Laura must not have been paying attention to the prayer because, as soon as it was over, she blurted.

"We should have a party. We could celebrate Daddy running for governor and Thomas' birthday at the same time."

"That is a wonderful idea!" Mrs. McNeil said.

Tommy and Marsha looked across the table at each other. The realization hit them at the same time. Thomas would be eighteen and eligible for the draft. He would, most likely, be called to serve in the war. Marsha could not stop the tear that escaped her eye and ran down her cheek.

"What is wrong, Mother?" Thomas asked.

"Oh, you are growing up so fast. It is a Mommy thing. Enjoy your supper. I will be fine." Marsha said.

She again looked across the table at her husband. He gave her a reassuring smile. She forced a smile in return. Mrs. McNeil did not miss the exchange. It was a reminder of her years with her husband. They, too, had a way of carrying on a conversation without speaking.

"We can have a hay ride." Laura planned. "The men can play horseshoes. I will make a list of games. Maybe we can get some people to bring their musical instruments and have a sing along. It will be such fun."

Laura's excitement was a welcome relief from the tension

of their lives suddenly changing all over again.

"Will we live in the city?" Marsha asked.

"No. I want our life to stay as normal as possible. I will go down to work and return home as much as I can. If I have learned anything, it is to delegate tasks to other people. No one man can do everything. I will set up an office here in case of emergency." Tommy said.

That brought a smile to Marsha's face. There was nothing about living in a big city that attracted her. As far as she was concerned, others could have the social scene if that was what they wanted. She preferred the farm and her kitchen.

The family finished eating and set off on their evening chores. Thomas grabbed the milk buckets and rattled off toward the barn. Butch, his collie dog, followed behind. Thomas had raised Butch from a pup and they were inseparable. He laid in the hallway of the barn while Thomas did the milking. Tommy poured feed into the hogs trough. They squealed and stomped to get at the food. Sparky honked his horn at Tommy as he drove out of the driveway on the way to work a night shift.

Tommy became lost in thought. The past swept past him. He thought of his first days in Hatsworth. There was the time Mister McNeil's mule kicked Aulding's car. He remembered learning to pick cotton with Marsha as his teacher. The day he sat in church and was touched by the preaching of Brother Newton came to mind, then. There was the day young James died saving his life on the battlefield. Swiftly the years passed. He ran his hand through his full head of hair, that he knew was fast turning gray. The bitter night Mister McNeil was killed brought a frown to his face. He had missed Thomas' birth but remembered well when Laura was born in their own bedroom. By picking potatoes with the Brown's, he had made lifelong friends. Managing the farm was second nature to him now. He kept his books meticulously. It was always a fresh joy to see the new born calves in the spring and the corn sprouting from the fresh earth. Even the winters had been wonderful, with the smell of fresh sausage cooking and the hams smoking in the smokehouse.

"What are you smiling about Daddy?" Thomas stood with two buckets of milk in his hands looking at his daddy.

"Oh, I was just thinking about how good life has been here." Tommy told him.

"We have had trouble." Thomas said sounding very mature.

"We certainly have had trouble, Son. Life is often full of trouble. We must grasp the good times and cherish the memories. Do not let the good times pass lightly. They will give you much pleasure when you are old." Tommy said.

"You are not old." Thomas said.

"I am getting there. Getting old is not a bad thing, especially, if you have tried to do the right thing." Tommy told his son.

Chapter
18

As Tommy was a transient in Hatsworth City, so we are all transients in the world. As much as we would like to, we cannot live here without notice of the worlds tragedies. Like a pebble in a pond, a ripple on one side will reach the other side with a gentle nudge or a wave depending on the size of the pcbblc.

Hitler tossed a huge boulder in the pond of the world. He was one of the men who took advantage of the economic upheaval in the world. He promised a better day for the people and many believed him. As for those who did not believe, he had other ways of dealing with them.

While the depression may not have caused the rise of the Third Reich, it provided the conditions necessary to nurture such ideologies.

Waves came against our shores from Japan and Italy as well. The world seemed to be in upheaval at a time when the United States was in no shape for war. Some said the war was a conflict of ideology. Others have said the war was all about race. There are indications that both problems existed. History and the nature of mankind seem to be the best suspects. Mankind seems to be bent on repeating all the bad things in history while they add their own latest ambitions and misguided goals. Fascism, communism, socialism and democracy armed itself in the second world war and turned

Europe into a devastated moonscape. The infrastructure was bombed and blown up. Sixty million civilians were uprooted either by force or to flee the carnage.

New words arose and planted themselves in the conscience mind of the world. Concentration camps, gas chambers, extermination camps, the SS, holocaust and many other words describe the lows that mankind can reach.

Hitler played on national pride telling his people that he would lead them to their rightful place as the rulers of Europe. Underneath his powerful and seemingly noble exterior, there was a very troubled mind. Like an artisan might use a tool to accomplish a good thing, a murderer such as Hitler could take the same tool and use it for harm. And so, he used Germany. They barely had time to rebuild their male population from the tragedy of the first world war when the second one reduced it until there were seven million fewer men than women. One estimate of the total loss of life due to Hitler's War was fifty to sixty-four million killed.

Young Thomas Bookmark was an artist and a photographer. Partly because his father was governor but mostly because he was very good, he had his sketches and photographs printed in newspapers and magazines. He did some weddings and family portraits which made him some extra money. By the time the United States became involved in the second world war, Thomas was well known in his trade. Like his daddy, he preferred being on the farm. His other work gave him cash money to sock away in the bank for the future.

Tommy and Marsha sat on the front porch enjoying some valuable time together. There seemed to be so little time to spend together. With Tommy away a lot of the time and the farm work to get done, the two had to make time for each other. Thomas had grabbed the mail from the box at the end of the drive. He got out of his car and thumbed through the envelopes on his way from the car to the house. He saw one that looked like a government envelope and automatically ignored it as his daddy's mail. There was nothing for him today. Occasionally, someone would send him a check in the mail for a job he had done. Thomas kissed his mother and patted Tommy on the shoulder as he handed him the mail. He went into the house and grabbed the milk from the refrigerator. As he was drinking a glass full, his daddy called from the front porch.

"One of these letters is for you Thomas." Tommy said. He had already held it up for Marsha to see. They sat solemnly as they listened to the footsteps of their son walking briskly through the living room to the front porch. Tommy handed the letter to his son and waited for him to open it.

Thomas read the letter in silence then handed it back to his daddy to read. He was to leave for military service in one week.

"You knew. Didn't you?" Thomas asked Tommy.

"Yes. I knew. The United States has joined in the war against Hitler. Without our help, it is almost certain that Great Britain will fall." Tommy explained.

"Well, duty calls." Thomas said. He turned and went back into the house calling to Laura.

"Hey Sis. I am going to be a solider. You get to milk the cows until I get back." Thomas yelled.

"No you're not." Laura argued.

"Yes I am. Look at this letter." Thomas said.

Thomas went through training with no trouble. He was strong and fit. He never mentioned his hero daddy but word got around somehow. It was not his intention to deny his dad's heroic service. Neither was it his intention to try to be his dad. Thomas was his own man and it was soon evident in his show of loyalty and sense of purpose. He was not in uniform just to fight a war but to help end the war and the pain it was causing people.

June 30, 1944
Somewhere in France

Dear Mom and Dad and Sis,
    The Vikings fought for a piece of beach property here, then later two brothers of noble position. England and France finally agreed to let it be part of France. Now we are here to take it away from Hitler. I had a choice of five beaches to land on, so I choose the worst one. Utah, Gold, Juno all sounded too far away from home. Omaha was my choice but the Germans liked it too. They had one of their elite divisions there called Panzer Divisions which can move very fast.
    I am hunkered down behind a German built fortification like the old Norman hedgerows, writing this letter. The farmers built these five foot high walls around thousands of their fields. Once we take the fortifications from the Germans, they offer good protection. We are taking a rest now before we advance to the next objective.
    General Eisenhower somehow heard (thanks Dad) that I was an artist and photographer. He gave me a commission to warrant officer with special orders to document the war 'where ever I see fit' which allows me to roam freely, even between units. I must be careful not to get ahead of allied forces though. I often have to put my camera and canvas away to take up my weapons. War is a nasty business. Why would we want to remember it? Perhaps, so we will learn not to do it again?   Pray that my hands would stop shaking. I want my pictures to be good.
                    Love always,
                    Thomas

Cherbourg, France
July 30, 1944

Dear Mom and Dad and Sis,

 I am standing at the top of Roule Mountain looking down on the town. Allied forces have secured the Cotentin Peninsula, thus protecting the English Channel from the Germans. Of course, they have other means of attack, such as the V-planes and U-boats. Bloody is the only way I can describe the fighting here. William Brown came through here yesterday. He has matured nicely. He is already a veteran of much fighting. I told him 594, from Sanky's hymnal, which is God Will Take Care of You. As tradition has it, he yelled back 6 further on, which is, as you know, Fanny Crosby's Blessed Assurance.

 I am hitching a ride to the front in the morning. The Allies are expecting a counterattack from the Germans to try to regain the peninsula. I doubt they can muster enough forces after all the bombs we dropped on their airfields.

 Well, I best get off the mountain before some stray German takes a shot at me. Do not worry, I am doing good.

Love always,
Thomas

P.S. Tell Grandma I love her.

Oh yeah. Tell Butch I love him too.

Although Europe probably would have lost the struggle against Hitler if the Allies had not invaded, France had a strong resistance in place. When the invasion at Normandy began, a force equal to fifteen divisions rose up from the homes, hillsides and valleys of France. The Germans, not only, found themselves confronted by a massive force from the coast but the resistance fighters rose up in terrible numbers all around them.

After being routed and pushed back from the beaches, German forces mounted a counter attack to regain the peninsula of Cotentin but were boxed in at Flaise. Thomas had gone into Flaise with the front edge of allied forces. He was sitting in a café talking to what turned out to be a resistance fighter when mortar rounds began to fall in the street and on buildings. He took shelter in the café with his new friend. The mortar fire ceased and they walked to the door expecting to see American forces in the streets. A rumbling sound gradually came to their conscience mind. Tanks were coming but from the wrong direction. An armored vehicle came down the street with a German standing up in the front. The German recognized Thomas' uniform and fired his pistol in the direction of the café hitting the door jam at his face.

The freedom fighter snatched him from the doorway by the front of his uniform shirt while firing at the Germans with the other. She lead him to a trap door in a storage room and into a tunnel under the street. He followed without resistance, not knowing what else to do. He was trapped behind enemy lines. If he had been under the authority of any particular unit, he would have been ordered back with that unit. Commanders had learned of his special orders from Ike and so let him roam freely. His unusual privileges had finally gotten him in serious trouble. He ran behind his rescuer like he had never run before. She was lithe and sure of her movements. Her hair, which had been bundled neatly behind her head, was now flowing behind her as she ran. There was no pursuit. They came out of the tunnel in a small valley that was more like a big ditch hidden by a grove of old trees. She stopped to look around the area. Thomas started to speak and she shushed him. She pointed toward Falaise. Thomas followed her finger and saw a German patrol parked beside the road. They apparently felt safe, for they propped against their jeep smoking cigarettes.

His guide punched him with the back of her hand and motioned for him to follow her. He followed, rubbing his shoulder where she had hit him. She was strong, he thought. They moved quiet and slow back into the woods toward the hills. She led him deeper and higher into the hills away from all roads and towns. He was basically lost now except for his guides help. He placed his hand on her back to stop her. She turned like a cat, her eyes wide, then relaxed.

"Can we talk now?" He asked.

She looked all around their position, then crouched beside him.

"Yes, but quietly." She instructed. She spoke English very well which was extremely helpful since Thomas knew only a few words of French.

"Why are we in such a hurry?" Thomas asked.

"You would certainly have been interrogated severely since you are an American. I could have stayed and pretended to be a worker at the café." She explained.

"You saved my life." He said dumbly.

"Your welcome." She said her French accent heavier than necessary. She turned to go.

"Wait." He said a little too loud and got shushed.

"Sorry." He said. She nodded her acceptance of the apology.

"Sound travels well around here." She explained.

"What is you name?" Thomas asked.

"Marie-Louise Zola." She said.

"Thank you for saving my life." He said.

"You are very welcome, for the second time. Now, can we go someplace where we might not get shot." She pleaded.

"I just thought I should know you name since I have had to look at your backside for the last hour." Thomas said.

"I am sorry to cause you so much pain." She said.

"I did not mean... I had to see where you were going. I mean you were in front. You didn't cause me any pain. I do not mind loo..." Thomas gave up trying to explain.

"You Yanks are all alike. Just follow me and look if you must but do not get any ideas." Marie-Louise told him.

Thomas started to say something agreeable but decided to just have a drink from his canteen and keep his mouth shut. Marie-Louise smiled sweetly after she turned back toward the trail to the camp of her freedom fighters. She had adapted a tough exterior since joining the resistance. Her mother had been raped while she watched and the Germans laughed. Her father was dragged off to a concentration camp. She promised herself that she would not cry again until all the Germans were killed or run out of France. Today's smile was her first real smile in over a year. She liked the American but could she afford the luxury of a personal friend. As she bent to climb the steep slops of the mountain side using her hands to pull herself along, she often looked back under her arm at Thomas. He was trying to keep his eyes down so as not to stare at her. He did have to look up, sometimes, to see where he was going and seeing Marie-Louise ahead of him was unavoidable.

They arrived at the camp amid pointed weapons. Marie-Louise snapped orders. "Check the trail to see if we were followed."

She was obviously the commander of this unit and judging from the quick response of the men, perhaps, of the entire region. They ate and sleep most of the afternoon. When darkness fell, Marie-Louise started loading herself down with ammunition. Thomas asked her what was going on.

"We are going to kick the Germans out of our town." She said.

"I will go with you." Thomas said.

"You should stay here where it is safe." She said.

"I have not been in a safe place since the day we landed." He said.

"Suit yourself." She said and headed down the mountain with her fighters in tow.

Thomas laid back from the group to take some

photographs. However, he kept his weapon handy.

Their first encounter was a German patrol. They ran to get ahead of the group. Marie-Louise showed why she was the leader. She dumped her weapons behind a tree and walked out onto the path the Germans would come down. She smeared some dirt on her face and mushed her hair. When the Germans came into view, she was on the trail in a provocative position trying to fix the straps on her knapsack. It was obvious to the German soldiers that this was their lucky day. They had found a lone woman in the middle of nowhere. She let the men get almost too close to her then she screamed a frightened scream and ran into the woods. Five of the men, including the officer in charge, pursued her into the woods. She ran to the tree where she had dumped her weapons and disappeared behind it. The Germans saw her feeble attempt to hide and laughed to each other. They continued after her with a manly swagger.

"She wants to play hide-and-seek." One German said in his native language.

The men neared the tree. Marie-Louise stepped from behind the tree and stood with her feet apart. One hand still hid behind the tree.

"Come here. We just want to have a little fun." A German said.

She put her hand on her hip opposite the hand hidden behind the tree and gave her hips a little wiggle.

"Come and get me-e-e-e." She teased. With that motion and remark in the minds of the soldiers, she raised the weapon from behind the tree.

The soldiers tried to move off to one side and raise their weapons but it was too late. The weapon in her hand shot flames from its barrel and drew blood from the two nearest men. Those trying to get off the trail and out of her line of fire met a barrage of gunfire from her comrades who were hidden along the trail. They stripped grenades from the fallen men. The balance of the German patrol came rushing toward the gunfire in a dead run to rescue their commander. They were met with grenades made in their own factories. It was over in a few short moments. The resistance fighters automatically gathered the weapons and looked for any intelligence information in the pockets of the men. Personal items were not disturbed. Had it happened the other way around, the Germans would have pilfered any watches and rings they could find.

Then they ran. They ran hard and fast stopping every few minutes to listen. They ran along trails known only to those who lived in the area, although the Germans sent out search patrols on a regular basis before the allies came. Thomas snapped pictures of the engagement and the aftermath. He especially liked the one of Marie-Louise standing beside the tree. They arrived at their next destination quiet abruptly. Thomas waited to see what was next. He chanced a look at their next target. It was a fuel truck. A distraction detail was sent around to the other side to fake an attack. While the Germans were busy, two men planted grenades on the truck. The fake attackers retreated leaving the Germans with a feeling of victory. A lone sharpshooter, placed away from their group, fired into the gas tank of the truck. It blazed up. The Germans tried to put out the fire but the heat reached the grenades just as they made their attempt. By then, the resistance fighters were already moving off to find another target. An American plane flew over, apparently inspecting the smoke from the burning tanker. The fighters hid in the trees, not wishing to draw fire from the passing plane. The Americans had no way of knowing who was in the trees and might assume they were Germans if they saw them with their weapons.

They drew closer to town. The Germans were again moving out of town, apparently ahead of an Allied counterattack. Marie-Louise and her group ran ahead of the Germans looking for the right place to do them damage. There was a narrow place in a road with a steep rocky hill on one side. They used grenades and rifle fire to disable several trucks effectively blocking the road for a time. Their force was too small to stay and fight, so they were ever on the move. By the time the enemy figured out where the attack came from, they were already a good distance away looking for another target. It was reminiscent of the frontier fighting in early America. A hit and run tactic used by native Americans and again in the Civil War by the Confederates.

They slept under the trees for a week. Rather, they rested. It seemed to Thomas that he had been running all his life. When he tried to sleep, an imaginary explosion would cause him to jump to his feet.

Marie-Louise stayed near him. Her nightmares were different. She relived the time when the Germans raped her mother and took her father away. She remembered the Germans coming after her but nothing else. Everything was black in her mind until she woke up in the mountains where freedom fighters had brought her. She knew something had happened to her because of the soreness she felt and some bleeding. Some merciful block in her mind, kept her from remembering. In the mountains, she learned to use every kind of weapon she could get her hands on. She would make them pay. She understood nightmares and comforted Thomas when he awoke from one.

"Do not stand up Thomas. A quick movement like that could attract attention. Here sit with me and try to rest." She said.

She put her arm around his shoulder and wiped the sweat from his brow with the sleeve of her shirt. She pulled him to her shoulder and he did not resist. Normally, he would have been embarrassed to be cradled in such a manner but somehow it seemed okay. Marie-Louise was a veteran of fighting and danger. She had strength that was only now beginning to shape Thomas. He did not feel weak because of her action and his submission to it. Maybe tomorrow he would protect her from some danger.

"Time to wake up." She said.

Thomas had slept too long. He thought that Marie-Louise must be awfully cramped from not moving while he slept. She did not complain. She no longer scolded him or called him Yank. She understand the importance of documenting the war so, maybe, future generations would not allow it to happen again. She gained respect for his bravery. It must take a strong man to face war with a camera and sketch pad.

Finally, the group headed back toward town. German tanks and equipment were spread along the way. By the time they arrived at the town of Falaise, the Americans were again rolling into town.

As they neared the town, Thomas and Marie-Louise lagged behind the rest of the group. They would be at the café when they caught up to them. The two passed an open door on a side street and froze in their tracks to the sound of a rifle firing pen hitting an empty cylinder. They turned to see a bulky German reaching for his pistol. Thomas stepped toward him and pushed the pistol to one side. He brought his fist into the German's abdomen with terrific force. The man buckled under the blow and Thomas hit him again on the side of the head and jaw. Like a hog at killing time, the man fell to the street. Thomas tied the man's hands behind his back then poured the contents of his canteen in his face. The German regained consciousness and Thomas helped him to his feet.

"I would have shot him." Marie-Louise said.

"He may have some information the Allies need. I will turn him over to the military police." He said.

"You may be right. I still would have shot him." She said.

"Marie-Louise. May I tell you something? Please do not be upset with me." Thomas said as he pushed the German ahead of him.

"Sure. Go ahead." She said.

"You are an extremely strong person. I admire you for the effort you have put forth to free your country." He started.

"And?" She asked knowing there was something else.

"I know people change in wartime. I am not the same person I was when I left home. Soon, though, the war will be over and we will have to try to put it behind us. I understand why you hate the Germans but we cannot go on hating every German forever. There are people of German descent who are fighting right along with Americans. The people who did harm to your parents and you may already be dead. Like I said, I understand why you feel the way you do. I have become very fond of you. I do not want your hate for the Germans to destroy you inside." Thomas stopped talking thinking that he had already said too much.

"I will try." Marie-Louise said. "Forgiveness is a hard thing."

Oddly, the German had turned his head to one side as if he were listening to the conversation. Thomas went to look for an MP while Marie-Louise went to the café. It surprised Thomas when the German spoke.

"I was a teacher before the war. I am glad it is almost over." The German said.

"You speak English!" Thomas exclaimed.

"Yes I do. I was in intelligence and will cooperate with your MP's. I am glad I did not shot you. I heard what you said about putting hate and the war behind us. You are a good man Thomas." He said.

"That is a big compliment coming from a German soldier." Thomas said.

"Think of me as a teacher. The war is over for me. You hit pretty hard. That is the first time I have been knocked out by any man." He said.

"It comes from splitting fence post." Thomas said.

"Like your Abraham Lincoln?" The teacher said.

"Yes." They approached a jeep with two MP's inside. Thomas turned his prisoner over to them.

Thomas showed them his identification, including the letter from Ike. They waited for what he had to say.

"This man is former intelligence. He speaks English and has said he will cooperate. Please see that he is treated fairly." Thomas told them.

They saluted Warrant Officer Bookmark who was obviously a friend of the Allied Commander. The prisoner would be treated fairly. Thomas extended his hand to the German teacher.

"Let the healing start with us." Thomas said.

"With us." The man said while extending his tied hands.

Falaise, France
August 13, 1944

Dear Mom and Dad and Sis,
Sorry for not writing sooner. I got separated from the Americans for a while and was fighting with the French resistance. The lady in charge saved my life. Her name is Marie-Louise Zola. I am thinking about changing the last part of her name.
They call this place the "killing ground" and for good reason. The Germans were trapped here after a failed attempt to counterattack.
I have to go to General Eisenhower's headquarters to delivery my photographs and sketches then I will be going to Germany (what's left of it) to take pictures of what they are calling 'death camps". Then I would like to bring Marie-Louise home to see if she likes it there. She should know by the time I get back from the Far East. I must have the only camera in the war. Anyway they want some pictures the way I take them. I should only be over there a couple of months.
If it is okay for me to bring Marie-Louise home to stay while I am gone, please let me know either way. I do not want to marry her and drag her away from France, if she is not going to be happy. She has no family here anymore.

Love always,
Thomas

P.S. I will send copies of the stuff I have done that is not classified. Please put them in a safe place for me.

Chapter
19

There is no way a young man could prepare himself for
what Thomas had seen and taken photographs of. The story
of death and destruction from Omaha Beach to the borders of
Germany was a gruesome tale. How could it be any worse?
Then, a jeep dropped Thomas off at an extermination camp.
He was appointed a guide with the rank of captain to escort
him.

"You should brace yourself for some bad stuff." The
captain told him.

"Oh, I have been with the combat units since Normandy."
Thomas replied confidently.

"I was at Normandy too. As if that was not bad enough,
Hitler has a secret that will turn the whole world sick to their
stomach." The captain said.

Thomas walked with the captain to a large mound of dirt
that had been push up recently. They were standing outside a
fenced camp, obviously some kind of prison camp.

"Down there." The captain pointed.

What Thomas saw turned his stomach inside out and
everything in it came rushing out. The captain offered him a
canteen of water. Thomas rinsed his mouth and washed his
face. He still felt as if he was too weak to stand. In a deep
trench before him were hundreds, maybe thousands of nude
bodies. Men, women and children all piled on top of each
other. Their bodies were emaciated with bones showing and
protruding through the skin. Thomas started to raise his

camera from habit but the water he had just swallowed came rushing up his throat. The captain placed his hand on the young man's shoulder.

"I am sorry." Thomas said.

"Nothing to be sorry about Mister Bookmark. I did the same thing. I would now, except I stopped eating." The captain said.

"Call me Thomas, please." He said.

"I'm Matthew." The captain replied.

"What happened here?" Thomas asked.

"Hitler hated Jews. He was trying to exterminate all of us." Matthew said.

"I am sorry for your people." Thomas said.

"Just take your pictures. Do not let the world forget what happened here." Matthew told him.

"When I get finished, no one will forget. I guarantee that." Thomas said.

He snapped photograph after photograph in death camp after death camp. He went to the gas chambers and torture chambers. He took pictures of former prisoners trying to find their way home. When he seemed unable to capture the extent of the carnage with his camera, he took out his sketch pad and made drawings complete with measurements where appropriate. He sat and listened to stories told by the former prisoners. These he wrote up and included in his reports. He acquired age lines in his face as many young men did in this war. His hair streaked with premature gray. He had already matured beyond his years since Omaha Beach but his time in Germany aged him beyond explanation. He doubted his family would recognize him when he got home. It was July 1945. Thomas had been gone eighteen months.

Thomas traveled around German taking roll after roll of film. Finally the awful task was as finished as he could stand to make it. He returned to Falaise to spend some time near Marie-Louise and to do further research on the French resistance. His photographs of the people of war torn France would be invaluable to restoration efforts. He left for Ike's headquarters with intentions of getting it over with as soon as possible. General Eisenhower noticed the change in Warrant Office Bookmark immediately. After he had looked at the photographs and sketches, he understood fully.

"You are ordered to return to the states as soon as possible." Ike told him.

"I have a special request." Thomas said.

"Name it." Ike said.

"I met a girl who has no family left. She is a leader of the resistance. I want to take her to my family to see if she likes it at home before I marry her. I have to go to the Far East. She should know by the time I return." Thomas explained.

"Of course. I will have all the papers drawn up before you leave. I am sorry you have to go to the Far East. It is not much better over there from what I hear. It seems all the demons have been turned loose on planet earth. I know why you are going to the Far East but it is highly classified. By the way, your authorization for your mission in the Far East will come directly from the president since General MacArthur is in charge over there. He may not like you snooping around on his turf and his adjutant, General Sutherland, can be very trying at times. Your reclassification to reserve status will be effective upon your return. You have done enough." Ike said.

"General, I believe you are correct about the demons and yes, I am ready to go back to civilian life." Thomas said tiredly.

"I am taking these photos and sketches to Washington in a couple of days. You and your sweetheart will go home on my private plane. I would like to hear more about what you have seen." General Eisenhower told Thomas. Ike called his aide and told him to get the papers Marie-Louise would need to travel.

"She will have a permanent visa and can stay as long as she likes." Ike told him.

"Thank you General. You have been very generous to me

and the girl I love." Thomas said. "May I say, I believe you have done a great service to our country and the world. I wish you all the best when you return to the United States."

Thomas left to get Marie-Louise for the trip to America. Ike sat at his desk looking through the photographs and sketches. He tried to imagine the danger and pain the young warrant officer endured to document the war. He could only guess. One thing he could do. Ike took up his pen and wrote out a glowing commendation for Warrant Officer Thomas Bookmark:

"For distinctive service during extreme conditions, Warrant Officer Bookmark is hereby honored for his valor and loyalty in the performance of his very unusual and important mission. Details of which are still highly classified. As the horror of this war is revealed, the scope of this man's exploits will also be revealed. He has been successful in documenting the latest tragedy of war so that we might remember and strive to prevent such future events.

His unflinching bravery in the most extreme dangers of the war have earned him my personal respect and I hereby recommend that each nation involved in our effort award such honors as seem appropriate."

Signed
Dwight D Eisenhower
Supreme Commander
Allied Forces Europe

A stream of medals followed Thomas until they finally caught up with him later. Governor Tommy Bookmark had the honor of presenting them to his son. A couple of the awards are mentioned here. The Nobel Prize would not come for a few years when his private publication of *When Will We Learn? Pictures of War* was published.

Croix de Guerre, known as the French War Cross was given to reward feats of bravery. Thomas' medal displayed the bronze star. The most excellent order of the British Empire honored Thomas with the Knight Grand Cross. Other medals of American origin were equally deserved and awarded at his homecoming. As many military men would attest, stepping foot on American soil was more prized than any medal.

On August 6, 1945 a B-29 bomber flew over Hiroshima, Japan. It became the first city to be struck by an atomic bomb. Hiroshima was, historically, a military center located on the delta of the Ota River. The immediate casualty count ranged in the area of 70,000 killed. Radiation has since raised the death toll.

Based on the knowledge available at the time, the area was declared safe for inspectors to enter. Thomas accompanied the team to take photographs of the aftermath. He scurried through the charred rubble of what use to be two great cities to take his pictures. In his natural desire to be thorough, he visited hospitals and the streets to take photographs and to draw sketches of those who were injured but had so far survived the blast.

Thomas arrived in Japan after hopscotching from island to island. He documented the bitter remains of war until he thought nothing could hurt him anymore. He felt all numb inside. His arrival in Japan let him know that he was not numb enough. There would be no treatment or antidote to cure the pain he felt. He had seen more of the two theaters of battle than any one man should have to see. Like a true professional he accumulated the photographs, sketches and written commentary that was expected of him. By September, he was on his way home, a far cry from the young man who left the farm only a couple of years before.

Marie-Louise had serious adjustments to make upon her arrival on the farm. She was a battle hardened woman. Yet, as she spent time with Marsha and Mrs. McNeil, she gradually let the tender person inside shine through. She learned to dress in the clothing a lady would wear. Getting to the point where she did not jump at every noise took longer. Her every sense was geared to survival in a hostile environment. She vented her anger from the war in the fields while pulling ears of corn and tossing them into the trailer. There was unceasing work to be done on the farm and much to learn. Marsha taught her patiently. Marie-Louise found that there was little time to ponder the past. On the farm, their actions were controlled by the seasons. In the war, their actions were controlled by the whelms of a madman.

Chapter

20

Tommy's last act as governor was to award his son the
medals that had finally caught up to him. Thomas accepted
them with his back straight and a stiff salute. It was expected
of him. In his heart, he only wanted to go home and forget the
images in his head. The photographs and sketches he had
made might fade or be lost in some catastrophe but the
images in his head would stay with him to his grave. He and
his father did not have long conversations about what they
had seen in war. They were, in a sense, two different kinds of
soldiers. The one plowing ever toward the enemy to defeat
him. The other striving to document a tragedy that should
never happen again. Yet, in war, there is no good job. In all of
them, people must die. There had developed a deep
understanding for each other, which did not need an
abundance of words between them.

They came back to Hatsworth together. The town was out
in force to welcome them home. They gathered at the old
hotel where one last ceremony was endured to help folks put
the past to rest. After the formal ceremony, Tommy and
Marsha stepped out of the way, to allow Thomas his reunion
with Marie-Louise.

"I am so happy to see you." Marie-Louise told him.

"What do you think of America?" Thomas asked.

"If all America is like Hatsworth, I love it." She said, "As long as, you are here with me."

"Then, we shall be married." Thomas said.

Laura was in hearing distance of the conversation. She could not be pried loose from Thomas' arm. Except, she did let go when he hugged Marie-Louise.

"We are having another wedding." She announced.

The announcement brought another round of cheers from the crowd. Even Butch seemed to understand. He jumped and ran around Thomas and Marie-Louise. Tommy put his arm around Marsha's shoulder and pulled her close to him. They smiled at the announcement, as well as, the exuberance of their daughter. Along with their rejoicing over their son, they wondered at their daughter's excitement and what was ahead for her.

Sparky stood with Betty and their two children. They were both girls and were dressed in pink cotton dresses. Their hair was held in place with pink hair clasps. Sparky glanced across the crowd at Tommy. Tommy nodded his head in response. They had come a long way together and found happiness in a small town.

A big man with gray hair made his way through the crowd. He appeared to be just another well-wisher. Boss Lipston had been in prison for almost as long as Thomas had been alive. It was a long time but not as much as he deserved for what took place at the McNeil farm. Boss did not blend in very well. While the crowd held their heads up and waved their hands, Boss walked and squeezed through the crowd with his head down and one hand in his pocket. He had many years to let the bitterness grow inside of him. More than that, he was a man very much afraid. He feared the day he got out of jail and had to face that country sheriff. He had no way of knowing that Tommy had long put it behind him. As far as he was concerned, justice had been rendered by the legal system. Lipston decided to just end it all by killing the sheriff, rather than face a life of fear.

Sparky watched the crowd. It had become second nature to him. Perhaps it was wrong when his wife was standing so close and deserved his full attention. Thomas was due every ones attention for the duty he had completed. Yet, Sparky saw something out of place. After he nodded at Tommy across the crowd, his eyes fell to the crowd itself. He spotted the man moving toward Tommy and Marsha. It just did not look right. He patted Betty and moved away from her, working his way through the crowd. He was directly behind Boss Lipston by the time Boss got near enough to Tommy to shot. He removed his gun from his pocket and pointed it at Tommy.

Tommy saw the action and gently pushed Marsha away from him. She started to protest but he pushed more firmly and so she moved away. Tommy stood calmly facing the big man with the gun. The crowd was at the peek of celebration over the wedding announcement. In the small world of Tommy, Boss and Sparky the world was in slow motion.

"You won't come looking for me, Bookmark. I intend to finish you off right here, if it kills me." Boss said.

"I have no intention of coming to look for you. Justice has run its course." Tommy said gently.

"But you said..." Boss started to explain.

"I said if you did not get justice in the legal system, I would render justice. You have paid the dues set out by the court system. There is nothing between us." Tommy said.

"You sent me to prison." Boss said, searching for a reason to pull the trigger.

"You sent yourself to prison. Now, just drop this whole thing and enjoy the life you have left." Tommy told him.

Boss felt cold steel at the base of his skull. Sparky spoke softly behind him.

"Mister, if you twitch, your brains will be all over the train tracks. The hammer, on my revolver, is already pulled back. Yours is not. Even if you try to shot my friend, you will be dead before you can get a shot off. So why try?" Sparky told him.

Tommy walked slowly but unhesitatingly toward Lipston. He held out his hand for Lipston to give up his weapon. Boss slumped noticeably and handed over the gun. Marsha stood without breathing. She had heard about her husband's bravery for years. Today was the first time she had witnessed it first hand. Thomas had turned toward the scene, sensing that something was amiss. Marie-Louise was ready to pounce. The crowd started following their eyes toward the drama that was playing out. It was quiet when Tommy spoke.

"Mister Lipston, you should leave town." Tommy said.

"You are not going to lock me up?" Boss said.

"No. We have learned to forgive. You should try it. Besides, you and Sparky are not the only ones in the crowd with pistols." Tommy told him.

Boss looked around at the crowd. He partly saw, partly heard as men and at least one woman put their weapons away.

"We do not carry guns to hurt people, Boss. We carry them to keep people from getting hurt." Tommy said.

"What should I do?" Boss asked nervously.

"Why don't you walk with me to the hotel? They have some of the best cooking in the south." Tommy said.

Tommy put his arm across the big mans shoulders and turned him toward the hotel. He handed Boss's pistol to Sparky. The crowd started buzzing again over the wedding plans. Sparky put his pistol away and stood looking Tommy. A former war hero and legendary sheriff walking with his arm over the shoulders of a former mobster.

Boss was a beaten old man with nothing but a wasted life behind him. Marsha walked over to stand beside Sparky.

"He is showing compassion and does not care what anyone thinks about it." Marsha said. "My husband still surprises me."

"I have seen him mad and I have seen him kill. I have never seen him hate another human being." Sparky said.

Tommy and Boss were almost to the hotel with the others starting to walk in the same direction.

"Boss, let me tell you a story." Tommy said.

"A story?" Boss questioned.

"A very old story. It changed my life. You look like someone who could use a friend." Tommy told him.

Miss Alice was not there this time. She had passed quietly to heaven after many years of praying folks through their troubles. Brother Newton conducted the services while Thomas was away. Folks were still talking about the funeral being more like a jubilee. "We will miss her" Brother Newton said, "but her prayers will linger with us for times to come. She fought her battles, not on foreign fields, but in the spiritual realm we cannot see. Her suffering has ended and she is home at last."

The words still bring smiles to people's faces when they remember them. Folks passing through might frown upon the little town and think it was protected from the troubles of the real world. They might wonder at the stories told by Doctor Hill and the dishwasher, Aulding. Some may pass by the farms in the county and feel sympathy toward the old farmer and his simple life. The sheriff could tell some tales, if he would talk about things. The young man with the gray hair at the local photo studio is courteous and known to be the best in the state. Yet, one would have to ask Doctor Hill about him to find out about his Nobel Prize and award winning books of war photographs. His studio displays only pictures of smiling children and an occasional enlargement of local history.

An old man sits in an upstairs room of the old hotel.

Sometimes he falls asleep during the day. He is still so big that he takes up all of the overstuffed chair. He has only two books beside his chair. One is a hymn book given to him by Doctor Hill. He told the old man that Miss Alice would want him to have it. He can often be heard singing the words to *Rock of Ages or Blessed Assurance.* The other book is a well-worn reference Bible lying open to Psalm chapter 40.

Epilogue

Hatsworth could be a lesson for all of us as we pass down the road of life. Everyone has a story to tell, many of heroic proportion. The gray hair may be a memory that still hurts. The limp, a price paid to help another. The transient passes through our space on his journey. If we are truly fortunate, he may even stay awhile.

> Hard times upon us
>   Let's not falter.
> We must take them
>   Like the horse the halter.
> We'll pull our load
>   As the Master said
> And trust his heart
>   That we'll be fed.
> If some days the trip is longer
>   Who are we to moan and groan?
> It's just one trip we must make
>   While He must hold tomorrow.

The End

Thank you for reading my book. For any errors, I apologize. It may not agree with history in every respect but I did draw from history and my days growing up. I did many of the chores such as picking cotton and potatoes. The old swimming hole is a real place. I hope I have brought some reading pleasure to you and encouraged a renewed interest in history.

Me and sister with the old faithful bike.

Me and brother with the cows.

Dad

The Author a few years earlier.

Mom, Dad and brother

www.ingramcontent.com/pod-product-compliance
Lightning Source LLC
Chambersburg PA
CBHW030332030726
47499CB00003B/738